SHE'S NOT BROKEN

**a novel
by**

KELSEY DAY

IYF Publishing, Beverly Hills, FL

She's Not Broken
A Novel by Kelsey Day

Copyright © 2018 by Kelsey Day

ISBN-13: 978-099987800-2

In Your Flock Publishing
www.InYourFlock.com

First Edition: 2018

Dedication
To Petri and Christine
You both know why.

Chapter 1

Melody had no reason to think this humid Thursday would be exponentially worse than any Monday. Sure, Larry had set the coffee maker incorrectly, so no magic brew greeted her in the kitchen at 5:00 a.m. She considered that an easy fix.

Sure, the power suit she had hung on the back of the bathroom door the night before lay in a wadded mass shoved against the wall when she got out of bed. She didn't let that ruffle her feathers; she had other clothes in the closet to choose from.

Sure, the trail of Larry's tennis shoes, sandals, and flip-flops from his side of the bed to the door had tripped her in the dark, leaving her with a bruise on her forearm where she'd caught herself against the doorframe. Life would go on.

No, the true morning firestorm began about three minutes after she'd handed a piece of paper to Larry, who sat in his La-Z-Boy recliner in front of a rerun of C.O.P.S. in the dark living room. Over the volume of officers shouting "stop resisting" as they huffed and puffed into microphones, she called from the open-style kitchen, "I have a meeting with the folks in data entry around 4:30 today, so Heaven only knows when I'll get out of the office."

He pressed a button on the remote to mute the television, bathing the room in blessed quiet, and popped up out of the recliner with more dexterity than she'd seen him display in months. His clumsy sort of pirouette to the back of the chair startled Sunny, the orange and yellow parrot trying to snooze in his travel cage on the kitchen counter. Larry's wobbly dance move also gave Melody a second to blink.

She glanced down at Sunny, who stretched his wings up from his back. His yellow wings with their green and yellow feathers made soft, papery sounds as he lifted them up, stretched, and folded them back down in place. The longer flight feathers with lighter yellow tucked back against his colorful tail.

"Do you really think this is acceptable?" Larry demanded.

Melody watched his face for a moment, discerning whether the shade of red was a sign of his high blood pressure marring another one of his poor pranks, or true anger. Larry's face had grown puffy over the past few months. His cheeks were rounder than they used to be and usually had a reddish tinge to them. The rounded portion of his nose tip had seemed to swell and remain a deeper pink than it used to be when they'd first met.

Even his ears, which were typically exposed by a closely-cropped, military-style hair cut, seemed to have fleshed out. This morning, it was all redder than ever, giving the gray in his pitch-black hair a more silvery appearance.

Behind him, the flash of red-and-blue breaking news bulletin on the television briefly distracted her from worrying about his blood pressure. It changed the color of the dimness behind him, adding to her confusion.

"You're talking about the list?" she asked.

He waved the paper at her, crinkling it in his grip. "This," Larry sputtered. "You can call it whatever you want to suit your agenda, but we both know this is an invoice."

Melody couldn't think of what to say. She wondered if the Neurontin and Respidol cocktail he'd been taking all week interacted with the Lisinopril to cause the paranoia bubbling to the surface this morning.

"Do you expect me to write you a check?" he continued. "Or am I supposed to go get cash so there's no record of my payment?"

"That doesn't make any sense," she answered softly, still confused.

"You've handed me a bill like you expect me to pay you."

"You asked me to give you a list of your half of the expenses," she mumbled.

She was dumbfounded by the argument. Three minutes before, she'd placed a kiss on his cheek, despite the smell of rotting feet that emanated from him, and handed him a paper that he'd requested. The evening before, he'd asked specifically for a list of household expenses, and he'd asked specifically that she include the homeowner's association dues in addition to the cable, electric, and water bills. She'd only done what he'd asked of her.

"Have you come unhinged?" he yelled. "Don't you dare turn this around on me. I don't know if you're laying the groundwork to kick me out or what, but don't make this invoice my fault. It's not *my* fault that we live in the most expensive condo in Southwest Florida. It's not *my* fault you can't afford to pay your bills here."

He smashed and crumpled the paper into a remarkably dense ball while he yelled. Sunny the parrot scooted into his cozy cave within the travel cage as if to avoid the noise.

"Don't make *me* out to be the bad guy here," Larry said. "You know I can't afford to pay all your bills for you. I didn't move in here to be your sugar daddy. I moved in here because you wanted a closer relationship. You wanted someone who could offer you protection. You wanted to live with a real man."

She flinched as the wad of offensive bills bounced off her forehead, rustling the wavy brown bangs she'd taken the time to style today. It wasn't every morning that she made the effort to play with her hair; the summer humidity usually ruined any fancy "do." But she had soft brown hair that waved just below her shoulders. It framed her oval-shaped face nicely,

12

adding to the professional look that her wire glasses offered. She didn't wear a lot of makeup, so the clean, fresh image worked whether she took time for hairstyling or not.

"Okay, okay," she said. "Look, I have to get to work. Let's talk about this when I get home this evening—"

"Do you really think that's the smart thing to do?" he asked.

She wasn't sure she understood him, but the idea of standing in the kitchen arguing about finances at 5:30 in the morning was akin to driving a stake into her brain. "I don't understand," she said.

"You're just gonna walk out in the middle of an argument? Can't take conflict so you're leaving?"

"I have to get to work. It's not a question of—"

"So *that's* why you handed this bill to me now," he said. He spoke as if he'd solved a mystery. "So you could hand me my bill and leave. So what's the deal? I pay up or get out by the time you get home from work?"

Melody put her hand to her temple, just above her glasses, trying to press a throbbing pain back behind her skull. "You asked me for a list of your half of the expenses last night. I got up early to type that spreadsheet this morning. That's all. Now I'm going to work."

"Yeah, you're sacrificing sleep to do this big favor for me, are you? You go to work. But don't expect me to be here when you get home."

Melody stared at Larry in the changing light from the television for a moment, considering his words. He stood before her in the same T-shirt and underwear he'd worn most of the week. The mustard from Tuesday night's corndogs and the cheese from last night's hamburgers dotted the musty clothing around his potbelly. The bruised-looking head of his flaccid penis peaked out of the flap of his boxers like a dead, baby bird. One hand rested in a fist on his hip as if he were a parent scolding a child. The other hand gripped the back of his stained recliner where random pop tart wrappers awaited her cleanup. From beneath the chair's torn skirt, she could see the round, gray lid of a plastic vodka bottle.

As she took Sunny's travel cage toward the garage door, she said, "Take that chair with you when you go."

She refrained from slamming the door on her way out to her car. After their first argument nearly a year before, she'd slammed a bathroom door in her old apartment, and learned the lesson that the physical release wasn't worth it. He'd lectured her for fifty minutes on the lack of maturity her display of emotion showed. She had to agree with him; slamming doors was not the adult way to express one's frustration.

Turning on the radio in the car so that some teeny-bopper song twittered over the creak of the rising garage door? That was a better release of tension. She closed her eyes and leaned against the headrest of the driver's seat, letting the words "we're never ever ever" be-bop through her.

Despite having achieved her fortieth year, she still enjoyed silly music sometimes. The idea that you outgrow bubble-gum lyrics or synth-pop or anything else that savvy marketers push on the masses as you mature was a fallacy. At times like this, she was thankful for repetitive, bouncy lyrics.

Sudden, firm banging on the window inches from her head bounced her right out of her happy place. Sunny squawked. She jumped, springing back to attention, and looked at Larry's red, angry face at the window.

"What?" she asked.

He pointed toward the dash, motioning for her to turn down the stereo. She obeyed.

"Are you going to roll the window down?" he snarled.

She preferred the muffled voice, but realized she only had to endure a few minutes of him berating her for leaving during an argument, and then she could pull out of the garage and drive away. She leaned forward to grip the hand crank on the ancient Oldsmobile to bring the glass down, and when the window was low enough, he reached in and grabbed her hair.

"Hey!" she shouted. Sunny squawked again from his cage on the passenger seat.

"Don't you dare tell anyone that bruise on your arm is my fault. I know you're out telling lies about me to make me look bad. Don't do it."

"Larry! Let go."

"Tell me you're not going to lie to people about me."

"Of course I'm not lying to people about you. Let go." She tried to get her hand between his grip and her head to relieve the pain of his pulling. "What is wrong with you? Let go of me."

He released her hair, but still had his hands in the cab of the car. His rancid breath hit her full in the face as he pointed out her ridiculous behavior.

"What's wrong with me? What's wrong with you, you big baby? I don't understand the way you're acting. You've been a complete baby for weeks, and now you're demanding payment from me and storming out like you don't care about us anymore. You're acting crazy. Like a child. Nothing but a big baby acting like someone's forgotten to change your baby diaper. You owe it to us to work this out. Call in sick to work and stay here to figure this out."

"Oh my God. No. I can't call in sick because you want to argue about money. I have way too much to do at the office today in preparation for the break—"

"That's right. You're soooo important. Just gonna leave me here with the strangers and let me figure out how I'm supposed to pay you."

"What strangers?" she asked.

He gestured angrily toward the condo door. "The strangers in the house! You know they freak me out."

Melody frowned at that. It was true he'd mentioned shadows and apparitions in doorways, but she'd chalked that up to heavy drinking. Of course, she couldn't use the words "heavy drinking" when talking to him about any shadows he saw. She wasn't supposed to know he was drinking again; she'd danced around the concept of his blood pressure medication causing the hallucinations instead.

She rubbed her temple again, and then turned the air conditioning up another level so the fan could move the stink of his breath away from her.

"Look." She spoke calmly while directing one of the vents upward so it wouldn't blow directly on Sunny. "The strangers in the house are figments of your imagination. They're from your blood pressure meds. Right?"

He nodded, as if he had come to believe the lie between them.

"Okay," she continued. "Each time you see one, I want you to think 'you're just my medicine.' Can you do that for me?"

He nodded again.

"All right. Now, I really must go."

"I think it's stupid that you keep taking that bird with you. Why don't you leave him here? I'll remember to feed him."

"We've had this argument too many times," she said. "Now I have to go. I have no choice. I'll be back this evening."

He nodded a third time, but said, "I won't be here if you think I'm supposed to come up with over nine hundred dollars today."

"I leave that decision to you," she said.

As she reversed the car out of the garage and down the driveway, Larry walked to the drive to stand there, wearing his stained and torn underwear in the pre-dawn of a Florida morning. Considering it was June, the number of neighbors in the community was low; no one would report him for indecent exposure. She rolled the window back up as she drove away, wondering if she could call that in anonymously.

Chapter 2

By the time Melody got to the office building in North Naples, she had five voice mail messages from Larry. She also had a co-worker sitting in her office. The dark-haired lady with the low-cut blouse and high-hemmed skirt leaned back in the ergonomic chair Melody had purchased for the office, filing her nails behind Melody's desk.

"Mels. You beat rush hour traffic again. And you brought Sunny again! How was your night?"

"Good morning. My night was hellatious. Yours?" Melody glanced at the bulletin board hanging slightly askew behind her co-worker. The tight gray office with its cubicle-worthy desk and hutch didn't offer a lot of room for moving around; a person didn't have to work too hard to bump into the functional things that lined the walls.

"Mmm. Not enough wine or chocolate," the lady said drolly. "Lair still seeing ghosts?"

"Yes, but with more conviction."

The lady threw her head back and laughed with her mouth open in a wide, round cavern of teeth behind burgundy lips. Melody wasn't sure which was worse—the sound of Betty's fake laugh or the fact that Betty had so little regard for Melody's intelligence.

"Can I have my desk?" She set a canvas bag on the end of said furniture. She still held her laptop bag over her shoulder and Sunny's travel cage in one hand. There was nowhere else to set the items until Betty moved out of the way.

"Yeah, yeah, but the staff meeting got moved up, so don't take too long in here."

Melody let Betty step past her so she could get around to the chair beside her desk. While she adjusted it back to a height appropriate for herself, she asked, "When did they change the staff meeting?"

"I don't know," Betty said. She waved her hand as if the change were a trifle. As if neither of them would get called into their director's office for a screaming match if they were late for a staff meeting. "It was in my email when I arrived this morning." She concentrated on the fingernails that matched her leathery lips.

"Great," Melody muttered. "Another failure of my email to forward to my phone. So the meeting moved up to what time?"

"7:30."

"I can't believe they call a staff meeting before the start of business in the remainder of the civilized world," Melody said.

"Welcome to the ninth level of hell," Betty said as she dropped into the plastic lawn chair near the doorway—the doorway that had no actual door.

"Do you know why they moved it?"

"Prob'ly coz of the break," Betty spoke to her hands.

Melody thought that sounded logical. She pressed the power button on her computer and listened for the welcoming chime. "The break," she muttered. "Whose bright idea was it to take three days out of the work week in the middle of summer?"

"Someone higher up wanted extra vacation days?" Betty suggested.

"Someone higher up doesn't have the work load that we do."

Betty threw her head back for the loud laugh again, causing Melody to wince. She wanted all the façade in her life to stop. Apparently, Sunny agreed because he muttered at Betty's noise.

"Is Chicago conferencing in for this?" Melody asked.

"As far as I know."

"Gawd," Melody said. "I can't believe those stiffs are awake at 6:30 in the morning, much less in the office to complain about how we're doing business here."

Ignoring Melody's commentary on the home office, Betty asked, "What's in the bag?"

Melody clicked through icons on her computer screen. "Scissors."

Betty bolted up straight in the lawn chair, nearly tipping it over and causing Sunny to flap his wings. "Wait. You brought us all scissors." It was an observation, not a question.

"Yep. Coz that's how I roll."

"O. My. Gawd. Can I declare my undying love for you right now?"

While the comment was sarcastic, it was honest in its friendship. Finally. Melody liked that, and she grinned at Betty. "Maybe I'll bring bricks of staples next week."

Betty giggled a true, entertained, schoolgirl giggle. She could be fun when sincere.

"Speaking of bricks, did you see the news this morning?" Betty asked.

"Bricks were on the news?"

Betty returned to the study of her nails while she explained. "The latest storm surge reports showed a brick wall toppling right over. Right. Over. The next storm is expected to get named within twenty-four hours and is on a path for Flor—"

The phone on Melody's desk interrupted Betty with its simple beep tone. "Melody?" an old woman's voice inquired.

"Right here."

"Finally. Melody, I must speak with you about office supply use before this morning's meeting."

Ignoring Betty miming suicide-by-gunshot, Melody asked, "To whom am I speaking?"

Betty's eyes went wide and she clamped her hand over her mouth to suppress genuine laughter. No one at Catholic Research and Publishing LLC, whether stationed in the North Naples office or the Chicago headquarters, could mistake Mona Avito's voice—or forced Manhattan accent—for anyone else's voice—or fake accent.

The ancient caller sighed heavily enough that both ladies could hear her disappointment. "This is Mona in the directors' offices. Can you come over immediately?"

"Umm, Mona, I'd be happy to, but I have something on my computer screen here that I've gotta deal with. Could we talk after the meeting?"

"Did you just get here?" Mona's voice asked. "I've been trying to reach you for the past hour. Dr. Mason wants me to get this resolved before the meeting."

Melody glanced at the time on her computer screen. It read 6:35. Her boss's secretary had been trying to reach her since 5:30 when she'd been standing in her kitchen arguing with Larry. She wondered how many people had jobs where the boss ordered a hit that early on a Thursday morning.

"Can you tell me what's going on over the phone?"

"If I must," Mona complained. "I found thirty-seven paperclips in your trash last night. That kind of waste is exactly what…"

Melody knew the woman continued to berate her for wasting company resources, but she heard none of it. Her lower jaw had loosened and slowly lowered until her mouth hung open and she stared across her desk at Betty. The two women shared a moment of disbelief, until Betty mouthed "thirty-seven" as if over-performing bad lip-synching.

"Do you understand?" Mona repeated.

"Umm, yes," Melody responded. "Yes, of course. It's been a bad week and I must have—I must have just lost track of my," Melody felt a portion of her head throbbing. Then she turned her body a bit toward the phone and said. "Wait. Mona? Did all thirty-seven paperclips appear to be in one generalized area of the trash?"

"What?"

Betty clamped her hand over her mouth again, and Melody found herself unable to look at her friend. Her own smile tugged at her lips.

"The paperclips," Melody clarified. "Were they all grouped together?"

"Well, I don't remember now," the voice answered from its metallic home. "That was last night."

"I see. I'm just thinking that I might have bumped my paperclip repository at some point late in the day and not noticed my clumsiness."

19

Betty moved her hand to slowly mouth the word "repository" as if it were the greatest word anyone could have pulled out of the dictionary at that moment.

"You see, I'm very conscientious of the company's need to watch expenses, so I keep a receptacle for reusable paperclips and one for reusable staples," Melody lied unabashedly. "If I knocked those dishes over, my clumsiness would have dumped all those paperclips and staples into the trash. What a shame. I'm so sorry for my clumsiness. Please let Dr. Mason know that I will be so much more aware of my movements in this little office from now on."

After a bit of stammering, Mona disconnected the phone with a short click, allowing Betty to release her manic laughter. "I SO want to be you when I grow up. But you know they'll never give you a bigger office, right? You're a woman and you're lucky to have an office at all."

"I don't need a bigger office," Melody said. "I need people to stop going through my trash after work."

"I hear that," Betty said. "Do you think she had that number written on a sticky note that she kept with her all night? And speaking of nights, tell me about Lair and the ghosts! Is that why you brought Sunny back again? How was your night with the ghosts?"

Melody grimaced. "I don't know what to do there. Sunny's with me to keep him safe from the *crazy* at the condo. Larry thinks I don't know he's drinking, so I have to keep up this act."

They both looked at her laptop bag as her cell phone within it chimed.

"I'm sure that's him texting me. He said this morning that he'd be gone by the time I get home tonight."

"Omigod, Mels! What will you do?"

"Fumigate the bathroom? Wash the bed sheets? Celebrate with a good-movie marathon?"

Betty gaped at her. "But, Mels. I thought you loved him."

"I did. I wouldn't have let him move in with me if I didn't love him. But that was nine months ago. Ten? It's like a freaking pregnancy. Time to push."

"I can't believe you'd say that," Betty murmured. "He's so cute."

"No. He *was* cute. He *was* interesting. He *was* kind. He *was* employed. He *was* part of the relationship. He *was* a gentleman. Now? Now he *is* a drunken, unwashed moron that sits in front of the television swearing about random things, expecting me to pay for his medications because he quit his job in a fit of anger and now has no health insurance."

Betty snarled as if seeing something repulsive in front of her. "That's so harsh. Isn't that part of being a couple? You take care of each other. When one of you is sick, the other steps up."

20

"Yes," Melody agreed. "And I have been stepping up, and stepping up, and stepping up, and I'm tired. I can't see how I'm supposed to keep supporting both of us emotionally and physically and financially."

"Sistah, Chicago's *not* gonna give you a raise just so you can support your boyfriend. How long has he been looking for a job?"

"I'm not expecting a raise," Melody said. "And he hasn't been looking for a job."

"How can you say that? He sent out hundreds of applications."

"No, he spent a couple months wallowing in self-pity when he realized quitting his job was a mistake, and then he spent a lot of hours one weekend filling out a few online applications for jobs he is not qualified for, thus no one granted him an interview, and now he's spent the last few months raging in anger against society. Even if he did get an interview right now, I have no idea how I'd get him cleaned up for it."

"It sounds like you're very negative," Betty said.

"I am. I'm extremely negative."

"How are you going to get past that?" Betty asked.

"I don't know. What I do know is I have sixty fewer minutes to get ready for today's staff meeting than I thought I'd have, and a ton of requests in the inbox."

"You're really going to start work this early?" Betty asked.

"I must."

* * *

Melody almost got started on the inbox upon Betty's departure before Sunny muttered at another interruption. She glanced up to see what disturbed him, and saw Patti Van Petten standing in the doorway. Patti worked in the graphic design division, and rarely spoke with Melody unless they were on a deadline with a project. To see the middle-aged mom this morning was unexpected.

"Good morning," Melody said.

Patti stepped into the little office and sank into the lawn chair. Her response was unexpected. "I have a new car."

Given Patti's flat, monotone delivery, Melody wasn't sure how to react. "Congratulations?"

Patti shook her head slowly. "It's in Chicago."

Melody turned her chair so she could fully face the woman. "Go on."

"I also have new furniture." She paused. "It's also in Chicago."

"I don't remember you going to Chicago," Melody said.

"I've never set foot in the state of Illinois in my life."

"Oh, no."

"About two weeks ago, someone tried to get a Wal-Mart credit card in my name near Chicago. The customer service agent called me to verify the information."

Patti's words started spilling out of her, rushing like rapids. "I looked into my credit. Melody, my credit score is under four hundred, so I started looking at what was going on and I have thousands of dollars in credit card debt that I can't trace, and then people started calling me saying they can take my house if I don't pay what these assholes have stolen from me. My husband has gotten some of these calls at his work and his boss is mad about it, and you know what Dr. Mason will do to me if these calls start happening through the switchboard here. I cannot cannot cannot lose my job, especially now that—"

"Okay, okay. Look, let's start at the beginning. Someone has obviously stolen your identity, right?"

Patti gulped back her panic and nodded.

"Have you flagged your credit reports with the credit agencies?" Melody asked.

"Yes."

"Awesome. Have you spoken to Mr. Marx in H.R.?"

"No. Do you think he can help me?"

Melody shook her head. "I doubt that man can do anything useful, but here's what I would do. I would protect my job by filing a report with human resources."

"What kind of report?" Patti asked.

"I don't know exactly. And I'm not saying this is the right move. I just think it may be a smart move to let them know what's happened and that it's not your fault. If the company knows you're trying to keep creditors from bothering you at work, then they really can't up and fire you for being bothered at work. At least, they can't fire you without you suing them for it. And Mr. Marx is at least smart enough to know that."

Patti sighed heavily. "I think that's a good idea. I should see if my husband wants to do that at his job. It's scary. You should see the bills that've been coming in."

"I'm sorry to hear it. Thank God the person at Wal-Mart was on the ball."

"I know. I think that stopped the fire from getting out of control." Patti gave a sort of scornful laugh at herself. "As if this mess isn't the very definition of being out of control."

Melody felt sorry for her co-worker. What a nightmare. "It sounds horrible, but this isn't your doing. Criminals did this to you. Do you need a lawyer to help you? Is it that deep?"

"I don't know."

"I have a wonderful lawyer who helped me through my divorce a few years ago. Compassionate and smart. He doesn't lead you on. He'll help you or he'll turn you over to someone who can help you. If things get to that point, let me know and I'll share his contact information."

Chapter 3

As Melody left the office around 7:00 that evening, she realized Larry hadn't texted or called for several hours. A sense of elation washed over her. Maybe he *had* left. She extended the passenger seatbelt across Sunny's travel cage and told the parrot, "We might have a relaxing night together."

Sunny muttered back, as if pleased with the sentiment.

She changed the station to 94.5 to hear more classic songs of the last century and sang along with the likes of Rod Stewart and Journey for the drive back into Lee County, thankful for the minor traffic of the late hour. Of course she could appreciate that it was crazy to be so hopeful at the idea of her boyfriend leaving. She cared about the man; she lived with him because she cared about him. But truth be told, the honeymoon was over. If he'd moved on, she was happy to let him go.

Then she turned onto her street and felt disappointment hit her as if she'd driven into a brick wall. She saw Larry standing on her side of the driveway, facing the condo, looking up at the roof.

"I'm not going to cry," she whispered.

Sure, she could feel actual pain in her nose and sinuses as if something had just smacked her in the face. She would ignore it. Sure, her stomach just gurgled as if she would vomit from stress. She could swallow the bile and power through the night.

"Hey, Sunny, he put on shorts today," she said. "Aaaand he got out his gun," she added. She pulled the car onto the side of the driveway without a man motioning at the roof with a pistol.

His bare feet and skinny legs looked like they belonged to an elderly man. They didn't look like they could hold up the rounded abdomen and thick torso of the fellow sort of standing, sort of listing to the side as he motioned with one arm above his head. He reminded her of the Time for Timer dude who hankered for a hunk of cheese from the Saturday morning cartoons of her youth.

"You stay here for a minute," she told Sunny, as if he could have hopped out on his own.

With the car safely parked behind Larry's, she turned off the ignition and stepped out. "Hey, Sweetie. Watcha doin'?"

"I'm trying to get them off the roof," Larry replied.

Just to double-check, Melody looked up at the roof. As she suspected, she saw no one there.

"Who's on the roof?" she asked.

"Those people. Get them off the roof."

"Honey, there's no one on the roof. You must see the shadows from the trees," she supplied. "Do you want to go inside and have dinner?"

He gave her an incredulous look, his mouth actually hanging open in the middle of four-day stubble. "What? Don't you see those people?"

Melody approached him to rest her hand on his arm. With a gentle voice, she said, "I think your medicine is making the shadows move. They're not actually people. Look again and you'll see what I mean. Do you see shapes of trees now?"

Larry shook his head at her. "I don't want to."

"Okay then. Let me take this gun—"

"No. I've got it," he said, holstering it at his belt.

"Okay. Now, let's go inside and I'll make some food—"

"You?" he snorted. "I'll cook something we can actually eat. Let me get the mail first."

Just like that, he was "back" from whatever fog his brain had been in. As he ambled toward the mailbox at the end of the drive, she closed her eyes for a second. She needed only a second to bite back any sarcastic remark. Instead of antagonizing him, she calmly retrieved her laptop bag and Sunny from the car. There was no point in trying to maneuver it to the other side of the garage, so she locked it for the night, and they went into the condo.

While Larry started preparing food in the kitchen, Melody helped Sunny get situated in his night cage. She whispered to the bird, "I'm sorry there's no time for playing. You're safer in here."

"I'm gonna put these on the grill," Larry called.

She heard the door to the lanai slide open, and then closed, and she felt herself relax.

*　*　*

By 9:00, she had eaten a warm-ish hamburger on a blood-soaked bun, taken a shower and searched for the mail. Neither Larry nor Melody mentioned the list of household expenses that had caused the ruckus that morning. Melody noticed that the wadded up list was missing from the kitchen floor, which probably meant Larry had thrown it out. She knew that meant it was forgotten, and her heart was sick over the missed opportunity to let Larry leave voluntarily.

Coming up empty on the mail, she decided around 9:00 to go to sleep, which was easier said than done. Larry had already fallen asleep with the television on in the bedroom. Sunny muttered in his cozy cave in the night cage, so she felt around in the bed covers to find the remote. She didn't want to risk waking Larry, but he slept with the covers piled up next to him, rather than on him, so she had layers to check. She couldn't find it.

"For the love of all that is good in this world," she whispered.

She looked up at the television that sat large and looming on top of the chest of drawers just a few feet from the end of the bed. "There's more than one way to skin a cat," she muttered. She got off the bed and walked to the television. She felt along the side until her fingers met the "power" button at the top of the machine. With a simple press, she bathed the room in darkness and quiet. Larry snorted and shifted, but didn't wake.

She climbed onto her side of the bed and snuggled under the covers as close to the edge as possible with a sense of peace and contentment. It was a blessing to sleep in darkness and quiet.

Sunny rubbed his upper and lower beak together in his own peace and contentment. The gentle sound of beak grinding made her smile. It was a blessing to be able to hear his happy sounds.

Whatever was keeping Larry from snoring at the moment was a godsend. She wanted to fall asleep before he started or else she'd be listening to that for hours.

The promise of sleep's forgetfulness began to seep into her, numbing her to worry and releasing tension from her body. Her muscles slowly loosened their vice-like grips on her bones, giving her permission to relax into dreamland, peaceful dreamland.

"What did you do to the remote?" Larry's voice boomed directly above her head.

Sunny squawked and flapped out of his cozy cave. Melody jumped to attention, every fiber on alert.

"What the hell?" she said.

"You broke the remote," he said.

"No," she moaned. "I turned off the TV."

"What?" he asked.

"I turned off the TV," she repeated.

"And now the remote won't work. What did you do?"

Sunny muttered as he climbed back up the side of his night cage to the cozy cave.

"Use the TV in the living room," she mumbled.

"I can't hear you," he said.

"Go watch TV in the living room."

"I want to sleep in here. I was watching TV in here. You screwed this up and now I can't watch—"

"Larry! Go to the living room."

"Fine. That's some thanks I get for making you dinner. You're such a baby. Gotta have everything your way. I can't have the TV on in the bedroom because you don't like it. You're kicking me out of my own bed because you don't want the TV on."

She knew better than to respond; it would prolong the tirade.

"Fine," he repeated. "I'll be banished from my bed so you can have your way."

She felt the bed moving and shaking as he climbed out. He slammed the bedroom door on his way to the living room, which caused her to jump again. Sunny fluttered his wings in the cozy cave, and she clucked her tongue to soothe him. "It's okay now," she whispered. "Go on back to sleep, sweet birdie."

Chapter 4

"I have to start checking this coffee pot before bed," Melody told Sunny.

The parrot looked up at her from the treat she'd given him. He paused only a moment, as if considering how the coffee pot might affect his day, and then went back to munching on the treat he held in his talon.

While she switched the pot from "brew delay" to "brew now," she glanced up at Larry moving into the living room with a blanket. At some point in the night, he had returned to the bedroom, awakened her with all his shuffling and shaking of the bed, and then snored for hours. She wanted the wake-me-up coffee before driving to Naples.

"I want to talk to you before you go to work," he said.

In her mind, Melody heard alarm bells clanging. On the air, she heard her own voice saying, "Are you okay?"

He dropped the blanket onto the La-Z-Boy and proceeded to the kitchen. He positioned himself between her and the garage door before he began talking. "I want to say I'm sorry for our fighting."

She watched his body language. He had put on the same cargo shorts he'd been wearing the evening before to come out here and talk this morning, so the stance of both feet firmly planted hip distance apart, arms down at his sides like an ape, was effective. She wasn't sure how to respond.

"Nothing?" he asked. "You have nothing to say?"

"I'm not sure what you want me to say."

"How about you're sorry, too?" he prompted.

"Well, of course," she said. "It's a shame that we've been fighting so much."

"I think we need to get away together for a while," he said. "Take a vacation. We should go on a cruise. I'll look at cruise packages while you're at work today and see what's available."

Being stuck on a ship alone with him for days was the last thing Melody wanted. She couldn't think of anything more disturbing. "I can't think of a better idea," she said aloud.

"Can you get the time off?" he asked.

"Well, let's not put the cart before the horse," she said. "You look at prices and what dates are available."

"It always comes down to money with you, doesn't it?" he asked. "You don't think I can provide. I'm not man enough to come up with the money for a cruise?"

Melody frowned at him. "I did not say that."

"You implied it. It hurts when you tell me I can't provide, that I can't hold up my end of things around here."

"I'm not saying you can't hold up your end—"

"You can't put the toothpaste back in the tube. Why don't you just go to work. Go earn the paycheck that I can't."

While his words gave her permission to leave, he still stood between her and the door. Then she remembered her car was parked in the driveway. She could go out the front door. The level of relief she felt at that realization startled her.

It was past time to make a change.

*　　*　　*

After her lunch break, Melody received a summons from the human resources department. Betty was sitting in her office, offering treats to Sunny.

"What on earth does Marxist want?" Betty asked her.

Melody didn't want to over share Patti's information, so she didn't mention their co-worker's possible report to the human resources director. Instead she said, "Maybe he's checking in on my paperclip use."

Betty laughed her fake laugh.

Melody began her trek across the publishing company's campus. She stepped out of the trailer that served as a temporary office building for the seven employees who had similar tenure to one another, but no working relationships with one another, into the bright Florida sunshine. The afternoon rain shower hadn't cooled the air yet, so she immediately began to sweat. Luckily, the solid structure that housed the human resources director sat directly across the street. She didn't have far to walk in the sweltering heat.

"Melody!" a tall man yelled out. "Hey, girl!"

To be kind, she waved at Ken Bilso on her way down the ADA ramp, but he was faster than that. He jogged toward her as he shouted, "Wait up!"

"I've been summoned to H.R.," she said.

"Oh, that's no good. Whadja do?"

"Apparently, I threw some paperclips away," she joked.

He shrugged and wrinkled his nose as he laughed with a smoker's cough. "That'll get ya fired around here. Hey, I've got a joke for ya."

"One I can tell to H.R.?"

He laughed again, wrinkling up his nose and tossing his head from side to side. "Better not! Check this out. Why do women fake orgasms?"

"Omigod. What?"

30

"Because they think we care!" He punctuated the word "care" with an exaggerated pulse of his shoulders and then laughed his signature laugh, rasping until he coughed.

Melody felt her smile tighten. "That's terrible. I've got to get going."

"'Kay. But don't share that one with Marxist!"

She let her smile fall away as she moved on.

Once in the directors' building, she snuck past her boss's office so Mona the secretary wouldn't intercept her. She signed in at human resources' front desk, got permission to go in, and entered Mr. Marx's domain.

"I don't have a lot of time," he began.

She watched the middle-aged man stack folders on a credenza in front of a window that encompassed most of the wall behind one of his desks. He hadn't turned to look at her yet, so she took the liberty of sitting in the chair that didn't have office supplies spilling off of it. It occurred to her that Mona Avito would have a conniption if she saw the other chair.

"I understand you want some time off to go on a cruise," Mr. Marx said.

The statement caught her completely off guard.

"I beg your pardon?"

"A cruise." He turned to look at her. "You need time off? Are you overworked and stressed out, Miss Share?"

"What? No. No, I'm not going on a cruise. I don't have time for that. I don't have time for the break coming up this month. Where did you get this idea?"

The man stared at her for a few seconds, and then stepped to his larger desk and sat down. "May I call you Melody?"

"Of course."

"Melody, we are a Catholic publishing house, and we take marriage very seriously here. If you're ready to marry your boyfriend, we are ready to give you time off—"

"Stop. Stop. Stop. What? Where did you get this idea?" she repeated.

"Larry came in to visit with me this morning. I'm delighted to hear that you're moving forward in your relationship. I have to say, it's quite a black eye on the publishing house that one of our employees is not only divorced, but is living with a man to whom she's not married. If you need time off to get married during your cruise vacation, I think that's stellar. We can get started on the paperwork to add Larry to your health insurance policy this afternoon so that goes into effect right away. He thinks the rate increase is totally manageable on your current salary. Just tell me the dates; I'll clear it with Dr. Mason. Everything will be settled easily."

Melody continued to stare at him after he finished speaking. She was unsure how to respond without jeopardizing her employment. Her mind fired plenty of inappropriate statements around, but she finally decided to say something that would put the fear of God in this man.

"Mr. Marx, are you telling me that you discussed my personal relationship and my salary and my health insurance premium with a man who is not listed in my personnel file as someone with whom such information can be shared?"

As she finished speaking, the color began draining from his face. He stammered a response. "Well, I, I, assumed that he, he is your fiancé after all. He has a right to know—"

"No, Mr. Marx. He is not my fiancé. In fact, it's my hope that I can get out of the relationship as soon as possible. I do *not* need any time off for any vacation. If Larry comes here again, please tell him that it's inappropriate for you to discuss personnel issues with non-personnel. Please don't tell him anything else."

"Of course. Like I said before, I have a lot to do. I don't have a lot of time for this."

She understood that she was being dismissed. She also understood that she had to deal with Larry when she got home.

Chapter 5

When she got home, the garage door was wide open, but Larry's car wasn't there. She knew better than to get excited. She pulled her car in on her side and took Sunny to his play stand for some exercise. While she put chicken in the oven to bake, she listened to music. It was nice to have something pleasant at a reasonable volume in the background. About twenty minutes into dinner preparations, her cell phone chimed that an unknown caller was trying to reach her.

For some reason, she answered.

"Is this Ms. Melody Share?"

"It is."

"This is Deputy Sheriff Simon Taylor with the Collier County Sheriff's Department. Ma'am, Mr. Lawrence Schmell Dos asked me to give you a call."

"Omigod. Is he okay?" Her heart quickened its pace; something had happened to him. She felt a pang of worry for a friend.

"He's going to be fine. He was involved in an automobile accident this afternoon and he's at NCH Baker Hospital. Do you know where that is?"

"Yes, I do."

"The doctors would like to keep him overnight for observation, just as a precaution. He's in room three thirteen."

"Okay," she said, more to settle herself than to acknowledge what the officer said. "Should I come down there? Should I bring him something? Does he need anything?"

"Ma'am, he should be sleeping for the night. You can call the nurses' station on his floor for more information. Do you need that number?"

"Yes, I do. Hang on just a second. Gimme just a second." She scanned the kitchen for a pen, and found herself instinctively opening the junk drawer next to the pantry.

"No hurry, Ma'am," the officer's deep and soothing voice said in her ear. "I know this is catching you off guard."

"Okay, I'm ready." She held the pen above the grocery list pad that was always, constantly, reliably stuck to the side of the refrigerator with a magnet.

By the time they finished the call, Melody felt confident Larry wasn't injured; merely bruised and being observed. Visiting hours were nearly over by the time they finished the call as well. There was no way she could drive all the way back to Naples, and then downtown, in thirty minutes. Instead, she called his room to see if he was awake. When no one answered, she had to leave a voice mail.

"Larry, a police officer just called to tell me you're in the hospital. I hope you get to rest well tonight. I'll be there when visiting hours start again in the morning. Sleep well, Honey. Good night."

She left a similar message on his cell phone before going to the garage to close its large, creaky door for the night. Seeing half of the space unfilled gave her an ominous feeling. This would be a calm and peaceful night with Larry's car, thus Larry, over an hour away in downtown Naples, stuck in a bed with nurses to fret over him instead of her. There he would get legal pain relief and, if he tried hard enough, he'd get attention from nurses or techs.

But the gaping bay made her feel somehow alone and exposed, as if she had more to take care of because she was the only adult in the condo.

Part of her knew she was always the only adult in the condo.

She checked the front door to make sure it was locked and the chain in place. She went to the back lanai to check the slider. It was not locked, so she fixed that and placed an umbrella in the track to make it even more difficult to open, should someone manage to break the lock. She closed all the blinds on all the windows that she checked, finding each one of them unlocked and in need of securing.

"It's like we've been living in a house that invited someone to break in," she told Sunny.

The parrot fluffed his yellow wings and danced on his perch to get her attention. She lifted him to her shoulder and together they spent a quiet evening.

* * *

Her cell phone began chiming shortly after midnight with Larry texting her. He kept up a steady stream of two to three texts in a row every five minutes. Like clockwork.

The noise finally roused her fully enough that she plucked the phone off the nightstand by her side of the bed, and looked at the too-bright object. Her eyes squinted on their own to adjust, trying to focus as she flicked the screen, scrolling up to see the initial message.

Vitriol filled the screen as message after message accused her of waiting (on purpose) until after visiting hours to try reaching him, and then accused her of wishing he had died in the accident, and then accused her of sleeping peacefully while he suffered in agony. She didn't read them all; just the highlights.

"Why did you wait until after visiting hours to call me?"

"Are you avoiding my question?"

"I know you're there and I know you're avoiding me."

"I could have died today and you couldn't even come to see me during visiting hours."

"I know you would have been happy to see me dead, but I'm not, so you have to come pick me up in the morning."

"How can you sleep while I'm in so much pain? You're a horrible person."

She typed back a message to the effect of "sleeping, will see you soon, my dear," and then turned off the volume and vibration. Sunny muttered his approval.

The interruption made Saturday morning arrive too early.

She found solace in having the house to herself. No one got in her way while she showered and dressed for the day. She took a minute to straighten up the bedroom, making the bed, complete with Larry's stuffed clown from childhood on the pillow. She threw open the curtains and blinds to let sunshine stream in.

Sunny squawked the sounds closest to "bath bowl," so she collected him to his flight cage in the living room and got a cool bowl of water for him to bathe in. While he fluttered and dipped and fluttered and dipped, throwing water to and fro, she gathered T-shirts and boxers from the guest bathroom, living room, bedroom, and master bath floors to the washing machine in the back of the garage.

It felt liberating to empty the dishwasher of the week's dishes and wipe down the kitchen counters so that area of the condo looked organized again. She folded Larry's favorite blanket over the back of his chair and fluffed the pillow he always held over his stomach when he watched television. She removed multiple shoes to his closet.

Before leaving for the hospital, she emptied the clothes into the dryer and pushed the button for that to work in her absence. She wanted to run the vacuum over the tile floor, but realized it was getting too close to visiting hours. If she didn't get in the car soon, she'd get an earful from Larry.

"Now, Sunny, I'm gonna go visit Larry at the hospital," she told the parrot. He clung to the flight cage bars nearest where she stood, his deep brown eyes staring intently at her while she spoke to him. "I might bring him home this morning, okay? Play with your toys while I'm away. I'll see you soon, Love. Who's my good bird?"

Sunny squeaked his special, short squeak that sounded closest to "bye-bye."

"That's right. You're my good bird. I'll be back soon."

She wasn't even past the guard station at the front of the neighborhood before her cell phone lit up in its cradle on the dash, reminding her that she'd turned it off in the night. She swiped the icon to answer Larry's call.

"Hey! Good morning!" she said with as much enthusiasm as she could muster. "How is my main man this morning?"

There was a pause before he replied.

"What was in your coffee this morning?" he asked. "Or did you get laid last night while I was suffering in here? Is that why you couldn't answer my texts? Busy screwing another guy?"

"Oh, don't be cross. How are you doing? The police told me you were okay, but I worried. Are you bruised?"

There was another pause. She knew she had him off guard. No doubt he was calling to chastise her, and her attitude was throwing him off track.

"I *am* bruised," he said. "I couldn't sleep last night. No one can sleep in a hospital. Are you still at the house?"

"No, I'm on my way to see you."

"Can you go back for a change of clothes? They're discharging me, but I need new clothes."

Sunny approved of Melody's return, and he squawked his happiness loudly. When she got back on the road, she called her friend who was supposed to meet her that afternoon.

"Hi, Inari, this is Melody."

"Are you calling to cancel?"

Melody sighed. It was a valid accusation. Since meeting Larry, Melody had become the friend everyone could count on to cancel plans at the last minute. The propensity for canceling, or for including Larry in plans, had limited the number of invites Melody received as of late.

"No, I'm not canceling. I wanna let you know that I'm going down to Baker to pick Larry up. He had an accident yesterday, so they had him overnight. They're letting him out now. I might need to be late this afternoon."

"Because Larry will require you to be late." It was a statement, not a question, and it was another valid accusation.

"Probably. But I'll text you if I'm gonna be late. Okay?"

"Okay. So was it drunk driving?" Inari asked.

"What?"

"His accident," Inari said. "Was he driving while under the *in*fluence?"

Melody grimaced. She hadn't let herself ask that question. She hadn't considered it. She hadn't even asked Officer Taylor what had happened. She didn't want to know.

"Ignorance is bliss," Melody said. "I haven't asked yet."

Inari made a cluck sound through her teeth. "Girlfriend, be careful. The museum opens at 1:00."

"Got it. I'm going to try for that time."

Inari ended the call. Melody didn't have to reach to touch the phone again. She tapped the steering wheel nervously. Inari was one of the few people she still had contact with outside of work; Melody didn't want to lose her friendship. Sure, Inari had her own psychological issues from past health and relationship trials that made her touchy at times, but she was a kind person. She had insight that Melody valued and respected. And she was a connection to reality that Melody craved.

Melody wasn't going to cancel on her. Again.

Chapter 6

Melody was far too familiar with the Naples downtown hospital parking garage. She'd had her own health crisis a few years prior, but overcame it. She'd brought an elderly co-worker from CRaP LLC to his early morning surgery here. She'd visited multiple older friends at this hospital. Since dating Larry, she'd been to this hospital's emergency room with him once during some kind of blood sugar episode.

In retrospect, she figured out the blood sugar spike was related to drinking, but at the time, she'd been sick with worry about pancreatitis. His boss at the time had not been worried or compassionate. Larry's illness and subsequent hospital stay cost him the job that Melody had considered a positive, stable factor in the early days of their relationship. His ability to get a new job with FedEx put him in a cute blue uniform and the "stable" category again for a while.

Now Melody walked into room 313 to find Larry in a more familiar uniform—boxers and hospital gown. He was standing next to the bed, pointing the remote control at the television that hung on the wall. She did a quick scan of him for bandages or splints, only to see a host of bruises along his left leg and more pronounced puffiness around his cheeks and nose than usual. His blood pressure must have been under control for the morning because he didn't appear red; he appeared kind of yellow. Even his arms had a pale cast to them.

A part of her body relaxed its tension upon seeing him up and alive, not hurt. She could reflect later upon whether that was self-serving or not. With him ambulatory, she didn't have to nurse him back to health.

"You poor thing," she announced, opening her arms to embrace him. She did feel sorry for him. No one enjoys being in a car accident.

"The nurses here are mean," he said, hugging her back. "They won't help me with anything. I can't get this TV to change channels so I have no idea what the weather's doing or where the storm's moving. Everyone keeps asking me to hold out my arms like they think I should have the DTs."

"Then let's get you home. I brought your change of clothes." She set the overnight bag on the bed while she spoke.

"Is there something to drink in there?" he asked.

"Do you want me to refill your water?" she responded, looking for the typical hospital-ugly plastic pitcher that should have been on his rolling tray.

"I meant vodka. I need a stiff drink after being in this place."

She looked directly at his face. "You've got to be kidding."

"Yeah, but it would be great to have a drink. Or three."

To keep up the charade between them, she waved her hand as if the conversation were a trifle, and said, "You know alcohol will screw with your medication. Let's get you ready to go home where you can be comfortable."

It didn't take him long to get changed out of the hospital gown and into the clothes she'd brought him. She smiled in approval at him in a blue, collared polo shirt when he came out of the bathroom.

"Why did you bring *this* shirt?" he asked.

"It's nice. You look handsome. Blue brings out the blue in your eyes."

She wasn't lying about that. Even though the whites of his eyes were somewhat yellowed this morning, the soft blue of his irises peaked through now that he was wearing the dark blue color. It even brought some pink out in his jaundiced skin.

He growled and sat on the bed to put on his shoes. "The collar bothers my neck."

"You're just not used to it," she offered. "You look very nice."

"I wouldn't think you'd like a shirt like this," he said.

She didn't understand why he'd say that, but didn't want to encourage something that was going to start a fight. Instead of continuing the useless thread, she asked, "Did the nurses give you permission to leave? Is there anything you need before we go?"

"I haven't signed out yet, if that's why you mean," he said.

"Oh."

"Remember the first time I was sick and you came to see me in the hospital?"

She smiled and nodded. "What about it, dear?"

"Jenny and her son had gotten me dropped off and you came to see me, all worried and lovey dovey. I used to think you were jealous of Jenny. You wouldn't care like that now, would you? If Jenny was here, it wouldn't bother you at all."

"I don't know how to respond to that. Jenny is your sponsor, Honey. I have no reason to be jealous of her helping you. I would be thankful if she were to show some initiative like that."

The lies dripped lazily from her tongue, and she wondered when it became easy to lie to him. When did she go from a kind, honest person to a woman who could deceive without blinking an eye?

It was true that she had no reason to be jealous of Jenny Hirpt. The woman was Larry's AA sponsor. The woman usually frustrated Larry to the point that he used the anger as an excuse to drink openly in front of anyone. But the idea of dismissing the dysfunctional relationship in a carefree manner bordered on psychotic. Jenny Hirpt and her son did more to damage

40

Larry and his chances for sobriety than the proximity of liquor stores to their condo.

"Yeah, you can play it cool," Larry said. "But I know you used to be jealous of her. I know you used to read my email and listen to my voice mail messages to check up on us."

She ignored the insipid allegations, wondering if they meant he was checking up on her email and voice mail messages behind her back. "You say 'us' as if there was a relationship. I have no reason to suspect you of cheating with anyone."

He snickered. "Because you're so good at providing sex," he quipped.

"Because you're a good man," she lied. "You told me that only cheaters suspect other people of cheating. I know neither of us has anything to worry about."

He frowned at her, but had no chance to respond because a young man in faded green scrubs walked in with a clipboard and folder, both full of papers.

Before they could leave the hospital, Larry had to sign a stack of documents. That took several minutes, and Melody watched him signing with no regard for what he signed. Then the intern turned to Melody. "This one is for you to sign."

"What is this?"

"He's being released into your care."

"What does that mean?" she asked.

"Oh, yeah, don't want to take responsibility for me," Larry muttered.

Melody ignored the snide remark while she read the paper the intern had handed her. "Does this give me permission to send him to bed without supper?" she asked.

The intern laughed. Larry muttered something under his breath.

Then she looked up at the fellow. "Seriously, what does this mean?"

"It's just saying you are the one who's driving him home. We have to release a patient who's medicated like he is to someone. That's you."

"Medicated like he is?" she repeated. "What have you given him?"

"All of that information is in his paperwork. And here are the prescriptions to fill on your way home." The fellow handed her a stack of light-blue papers.

"Omigod," she said. "How many prescriptions are here?"

"I didn't count them," the intern said.

She frowned at him. "Is this safe? This is a lot of medication. He's already on a few. Won't all this mess with him?"

"You can talk to his doctor about that."

She glanced at the white board on the wall, looking for the doctor's name. "Which doctor do I ask for?"

"Whichever one is on his release papers," the intern droned. "Or on the prescriptions. If you'll sign the release papers, you'll be ready to go."

"Wait a minute," she said. "You don't know which doctor has been treating him?"

"You're being difficult," Larry suggested.

"We have several doctors on shift overnight," the intern explained. "If you just sign—"

"I'm not signing anything until I get some answers."

"Just sign the form so we can go," Larry said.

"No. This is crazy. Look at this stack of scripts someone expects you to take. Someone expects you to have the money to fill."

"Ah, there it is," Larry said. "Money."

She closed her eyes for a second to calm herself, and then looked directly at the intern. "Bring me a doctor, or I leave him here with all these papers and he's *your* responsibility."

"You can't do that," Larry said.

"Ma'am, he's been discharged."

"I don't care. Bring me a doctor, or watch me walk out the door."

The intern stared at her for a second, as if gauging whether or not he could trust her. Then he left the room.

Larry took hold of her arm and spoke lowly as if someone else could be listening in. "You're embarrassing me. I just want to leave. Let's take these papers and go."

"Larry. No. Can you not see that this is dangerous?" She shook the stack of papers to make her point. "There are at least six or seven scripts here. Add that to the three you're already on. Do you really think it's safe to take ten medications at a time? You already see ghosts in our house. What will an extra seven drugs do to you? How does a car accident make it necessary to take seven drugs?"

"You're asking too many questions that are none of your business. Let's just go."

She pressed her lips together and pulled her arm out of his grip while she thought of how to respond to that. "None of my business. Like scheduling a vacation for me through my human resources director is none of *your* business?"

He stared at her in utter confusion. He truly didn't know what she was talking about. "Are you crazy?" he asked.

She shook her head. "Never mind. That's something you don't have to worry about. Let's just make sure the doctors haven't prescribed anything that will react wrong with the stuff you already take—"

"They're doctors. They know better what they're doing than you do."

"Did you tell them that you take Neurontin?"

He didn't answer. In fact, he looked confused again.

42

"Uh-huh. And did you tell them that you take Respidol?"

"I think I told them that," he said, as if catching up to the conversation.

"Then why is this script on top here for Reocyte?" she asked.

"I don't know. But the doctors do. It's their job to know. They're the ones who went to school for years for this stuff, not you. Stop going through my stuff." He took the stack of papers from her. "I'll get these filled."

"How?" she asked.

"Back to money?" he asked.

"This time, yes. Yes, I want to know how you think you're going to pay for six or seven prescriptions on the way home this morning."

"I don't know," he admitted.

The intern poked his head back in the room then. "Dr. Blainte went home when his shift ended. If you like, I can have him give you a call when he comes in this evening."

Melody felt defeated. Again.

"That'll be great," she said, knowing full well no doctor would call them on a Saturday night. She didn't even care to continue the charade by leaving Larry's phone number with the intern. She was ready to leave.

* * *

One of the other patients being discharged that morning gave them a tip for a low-cost pharmacy where most Medicaid recipients filled prescriptions for prices below the chain store prices. Considering Larry didn't even have Medicaid to help him, Melody and Larry thought a low-cost pharmacy sounded like a winning idea, and they followed the Good Samaritan's directions for finding the small brick building in a sketchy part of East Naples.

They locked the Oldsmobile's doors and went to stand in line to drop off the prescriptions. Then they sat in silence while the pharmacist worked on the order.

Melody had misjudged the number. There were actually eight prescriptions to fill, from two doctors. The pharmacist called her up to let her know the total would be around two hundred and seventy dollars. The Buprenorphine was free, but the Suboxone would be one dollar per pill for a thirty-day supply if they were filling both scripts at the same time. She sighed at the names of the drugs, knowing she'd have to pretend that she was ignorant of their uses.

The pharmacist also cautioned her against letting the patient use the Fentanyl patch and take any of the Vicodin tabs while starting the Buprenorphine regimen. "Make sure he reads all the warnings, Ma'am."

"I will," she said.

She didn't argue any further with anyone, but sat quietly when Larry said he wanted to go to the gas station on the corner to get a coffee for her. She knew that was code for getting alcohol for him. Given the tremors starting in his arms and hands, she wasn't going to fight it. She thanked him for his thoughtfulness and waited.

She waited and watched out the pharmacy window. Not many people were out and wandering in the heat and humidity of the morning. The few people she saw were either stopped to fill up at the gas station where her boyfriend no doubt guzzled a bottle of booze in the bathroom, or were going directly into shops for the relief of the air conditioning.

Movement on the sunny sidewalk caught her eye, and she watched a dark caterpillar undulating alongside one of many cracks. The pavement had to be hot on his tiny feet. From her distance, she couldn't tell what kind of caterpillar it was, but it crawled in its wavy fashion, slowly creeping along its lonely path.

She wondered if it would get to a grassy spot before succumbing to the heat of the sun, before giving up from the heat of its surroundings. Baked caterpillar would make an easy meal for a bird passing by.

"What a shame," she whispered. She took pity on the tiny creature. Grabbing a pamphlet from the pharmacy counter, she went outside and scooped up the little bug.

Its body wasn't as dark as she had first thought. It just appeared dark against the bright white-and-gray concrete that reflected radiant heat into the worm. Its spikes of burnt-sienna fuzz stuck out at crazy angles from an orange-brown body. Its eyes appeared darker brown than the body now that she was close enough to investigate. It continued undulating along the paper as if not noticing the change in substrate.

"Hang on, dude. Let's find you some grass."

She glanced up the street where she saw a potted plant next to a young tree sticking out of a landscaping grate. "Or a tree."

Larry crossed the street toward her as she lifted the paper to a lower branch. The caterpillar crawled onto the branch easily, still seeming to notice no change in its surroundings.

"What are you doing?" Larry asked.

"Moving a bug."

"You're such a freak. He's just gonna die when the storm hits. Here's your coffee."

"Thank you."

* * *

With seven new bottles of pills and a flat box of pain patches in hand, they headed north for their condo in Cape Coral well before noon.

"Do you want me to stop to grab a hamburger or something on the way home?" she asked.

"No, I don't want a hamburger. I'd rather sit down somewhere and eat."

"I have to get back to Naples by 1:00, so I need to drop you at home for lunch."

"What are you doing in Naples today? You don't have to work on a Saturday, do you?"

"No, I'm meeting Inari at the Holocaust Museum."

"Yeah, because that's a good time," he said sarcastically. "I think you look for any excuse you can find to get away from me."

"I invited you to come with us. You're still welcome to join us." She knew he'd decline, and he'd end up staying home with Sunny. As much as she dreaded subjecting her friends to Larry's moods, she dreaded leaving her beloved pet with his moods even more. So she added, "Then Mark won't feel out of place with us girls."

"Wait a minute. Who's Mark? Is that her boyfriend? You didn't tell me her boyfriend was joining you. Why didn't you mention this before?"

"The accident yesterday has upset your memory," she provided.

"Yeah, I should come with you. I don't need you getting involved with some other guy. That's happened to me before, you know. Carrie decided she liked some other guy's cock more than mine and everything went downhill from there. It's how I ended up in Florida to get away from what she put me through."

She pressed her lips together to keep from reminding him of his own mantra: only cheaters suspect others of cheating. It was a refrain he sang to keep her from questioning him when he was out drinking. Or carousing. Or whatever he did when she was supposed to trust him.

The last thing she intended to do while driving for an hour with him was start a fight. She'd unknowingly done that when leaving on a business trip once, and the drive to the airport had been interminable. It was far easier to keep her mouth shut. Her brain had successfully downplayed how he'd cursed at her for close to an hour, nonstop, on that drive. She couldn't even remember why he was mad that day. Something had happened that made him want her to stay home rather than go to a conference where there would be men in attendance. She remembered reaching for her keys in the ignition when she pulled up to the curb at the airport, and he reached over from the passenger seat and grabbed them first. She'd been stunned by how he'd timed it.

She'd also been eternally grateful to her friend for keeping Sunny that weekend while she was gone. And maybe that was part of the reason for his anger; she'd taken Sunny to a pet sitter, implying he couldn't care for a bird while she was out of town. It had been a long ride to the airport.

"You know, I could have died yesterday," he said.

The announcement was as startling as the break in the silence.

"Honey, you can't dwell on that," she said, still recovering from the disturbing memory. "You're here now and that's something to be thankful for."

"But what if the car that hit me had been going faster?"

She thought about how to respond to that. "You probably would have needed another day at the hospital, right? But we can't dwell on what *could* have happened. I don't even know what *did* happen. You say a car hit you?"

"You think it was my fault?" he bristled.

"I'm asking what happened."

"I assumed the police would've told you."

"Nobody has told me anything other than your condition last night."

"Oh." He seemed to think on that for a minute. "Well, I'm lucky to be alive. If the lady that hit me had been going any faster, it would've been a lot worse. As it is, I'm sure the car is totaled. The insurance better give me a new one. You know I wanted to give that car to Paula for her graduation. Now I can't. It's ruined. It'll probably cost more than it's worth to fix."

She thought that was the definition of "totaled," but she wasn't going to interrupt him.

"I don't know how to convince my daughter that I'm not a deadbeat. Yesterday made me realize, if I die, no one will come to my funeral, not even Paula. You, on the other hand, have a whole family out West and friends everywhere. When you die, you'll have hundreds of people at your funeral. People love you. Nobody loves me enough to show up."

"Gawd. *I* love you. No matter how immature Paula's acting right now, she does love you; you're her dad. What on earth have you been thinking about?"

"Seriously, don't you expect to have a lot of people at your funeral?" he asked.

"I haven't thought about it," she said.

"Well, think about it. You'll have half the country show up for you. I'll have no one."

They were quiet for a moment. Melody felt some sympathy for him, but also felt like he was overplaying the effects of the accident. She finally said, "You'll have me, Honey."

Chapter 7

While Larry got himself cleaned up and a pain patch applied to his hip area, Melody folded his laundry in the living room where she could interact with Sunny for a few minutes. She told the parrot they'd be gone for most of the afternoon, which seemed to meet with his approval only after his tray was changed and some treats were offered.

When Larry stepped into the living room, he said, "So I'm gone for a day and you wash all my things? Am I that gross?"

"It's standard practice to do laundry before a storm. Say, 'Thank you, Melody.' And put these in your drawer."

He took the stack of boxers from her, but set them on the bed instead of putting them away. It was faster to just set them down, so they could get going. "Did you call your friend to tell her we'd be late?"

"Yes."

"Is she mad?" he asked. "I remember her being uppity."

"She's not mad and she's not uppity."

"Well, *someone* is."

"Are you ready to go?" she asked.

"Almost." He walked across the house to the den, and let out an expletive a moment later.

Melody checked the lock on Sunny's flight cage to make sure her bird was safe from whatever mood swing was about to greet them.

A few minutes later, Larry emerged from the den and asked, "Why was the window in my den locked? Did you go in there while I was in the hospital?"

"I checked all the windows while you were in the hospital."

"That doesn't answer either of my questions. Why was the window locked?"

"I locked it so no one would open it from the outside," she said.

"What were you doing in my den?"

"I just told you. I checked *all* the windows. None of them were locked. Why do you care if I was in the den? Why are you opening a window when it's over ninety degrees outside?"

"So now you think I can't protect our home? It's my fault that the windows aren't locked around here? I swear, you think I can't do anything."

"I locked the windows," she repeated. "That's all."

"Because you think I can't protect us," he said.

"Because I don't want either of us to *have* to protect us. How's that?"

"That doesn't make any sense," he said.

She stopped arguing. There was no point in trying to reason with him or make him understand that it's easier to keep thieves out of a house than to subdue them or shoot them once they're in a house. She wanted to rail at him and tell him that she believed he wanted to shoot a thief, that he left doors and windows open to invite someone in for the shooting. Of course, such an idea was silly.

She hoped.

She still wondered why he needed to open a window in the middle of the day. He typically had a fit if she wished to open windows in the evenings when temperatures fell and cool breezes moved across the Cape. She would be able to smell it if he were smoking again, so she was confident he wasn't trying to get a couple of puffs out the den window—or any other window for that matter—while she was in the house. She chalked it up to just another oddity and dropped the subject. Before they went to the car, she snuck back into the den to lock the window, though. She wasn't leaving it available for intrusion while Sunny was in the house alone.

*　*　*

Inari and Mark arrived at the museum before them; despite having waited until they got a confirmation call from Melody that she had passed Immokalee Road and was headed south on Tamiami Trail.

"We had to stop for gas," Melody explained, trying to laugh off being late. "Had an extra trip to and from Naples this morning."

"Sorry if my *car accident* caused you any inconvenience," Larry said.

Inari didn't smile. "Oh goodie. I see you brought him along."

"Great to see you, too," Larry said.

Mark held out his hand to shake Larry's. "Good to see you again, Larry. Inari says you got banged up yesterday. Did it total your car?"

The juxtaposition of Mark's reasonable height, reasonable build, reasonable clothing, clean-shaven face, and reasonable smile against Larry's frumpy look overall startled Melody. Larry's 5-foot-8 height looked smaller than usual today. His skinny legs looked more toothpick-like trying to support his bloated torso. He was all wrong next to her. She didn't look at men as objects; that wasn't her nature. But she could see the blatant difference in images here.

She had originally fallen for Larry because he made her laugh, he spoke to her like a gentleman, and he had a good job. He smacked of stability and kindness back then. He was attractive to her back then not because he was some kind of underwear model—because, truth be told, even when he'd been working out, he didn't have an underwear model's look. He was attractive to her back then because he was a nice guy with a nice manner. All that was gone, and seeing the right qualities in Mark's outgoing smile was a stark contrast.

Mark's affable nature put the situation at ease, and the four managed to act kindly toward one another before entering the Holocaust Museum. It was a place of remembrance and reflection; they didn't need anyone making a scene. The few people moving quietly and slowly among the displays didn't acknowledge the newcomers that had entered their midst.

Melody and Inari stopped for an extended period of time in front of a particular set of pictures of families and children. They stared into the faces of people who had likely died after giving their images for history, after giving their images so the world would not forget the steps into true evil.

"It puts our problems into perspective," Inari said softly.

"Hey!" Larry startled them. Both ladies jumped at his sudden voice behind them. "I'm going to the gas station right up the road there to use the restroom. I'll be back in a minute."

"You're walking all that way in this heat?" Melody asked quietly.

"There's a restroom here," Inari whispered. (She didn't know the code.)

"Someone's in this one," he lied. "I'm taking the car." He jangled his set of keys and turned to leave.

"Don't wreck it," Inari said under her breath.

He flipped her off as he passed a man with a teenage son, but he seemed oblivious to the pair. At least, Larry pretended to be oblivious to his poor example in front of the boy.

Melody looked back at the pictures, willing one of the gaunt, black-and-white women to speak to her. She stared into the woman's eyes as if the deep-set fear there would offer some kind of answer, some kind of remedy, some kind of solution from ages past to apply now. She wanted to ask the woman of 1940, *"How do we let ourselves become desensitized to the wrong around us?"*

Melody noticed Inari pressed a tissue into her hand, bringing her back to 2018.

"You ready to head out to an early dinner?" Inari asked.

Melody nodded.

They located Mark near an exhibit of a Nazi soldier uniform. He acknowledged them as they approached and spoke quietly, "Doesn't it look small? Like the guy who wore it was a short little punk?"

Melody liked that idea.

"We're thinking it's time to go to dinner," Inari said.

He looked at his watch as they moved toward the front doors. He still kept his voice lowered as they passed an older couple reading a display of Post-it™ notes. "You'll run into the early-bird-special diners. Old folks with dentures sitting next to their bowls. Curmudgeons who can't hear each other. That sort of thing."

"We're willing to risk it," Inari said. "You want to go up to Zen?"

"Great idea," Mark said. "Have you been there?" he asked Melody.

"I don't think so. Is it Pad Thai? I don't think Larry likes Pad Thai anymore."

"It's a bit of anything and everything Asian," Mark said.

"They've got a sushi bar," Inari prodded.

"Oh, Larry loves sushi."

"Then it's settled," Mark decided. "Where'd he go?"

"Gas station," Inari said. "He has her car so he can meet us up there."

Mark nodded. "You wanna ride with us?"

To any normal person, the arrangement made perfect sense. But Larry would see this as betrayal. Abandonment. He would find a way to turn this into her preferring to be with Mark over him. Melody's hesitation caused Inari to roll her eyes.

"Gawd. Give me your phone," Inari said.

"No," Melody said. "I'll text him."

"All right. Just tell him it's on 41, by the 7-11 station about two blocks south of Immokalee. He can't miss it."

"You overestimate his skills of observation," Melody said. She started typing away at her phone while Inari guided her to Mark's car. Melody was a boss when it came to crafting a nonchalant text.

Within seconds she had something snarky back from him. It suggested they go to Olive Garden.

"No," Mark said, starting the car. "This one hates that place."

Inari nodded her head while she turned the car stereo down to almost inaudible. They could talk to one another without yelling. "I've sworn off Olive Garden since I found the plastic wrapper in my chicken Alfredo," she said.

"Ewww."

"Exactly," Inari agreed. "Tell him we're already in the car headed north."

Melody was afraid to say out loud that the couple's carefree demeanor was going to get her a lecture during her drive home; if not while at the restaurant in front of everyone. She typed her message and set the phone on the car seat next to her. The stress was eating her stomach.

"You know what you need?" Inari asked.

"A way out," Melody muttered.

She didn't notice Mark shoot a worried glance at her in the rearview mirror.

"You need to go on a cruise," Inari said.

50

Melody almost choked on air. "What? You've got to be joking. Larry suggested that very thing not even a week ago."

"Not with him," Inari said. "You need a cruise with you and one or two gals."

Melody saw a lineup in her mind of the girlfriends who would still be willing to go on a vacation with her. The lineup consisted of one woman, Julia, who currently lived half a continent away. No one else would put up with her for days.

"Calm and stressless," Inari was still saying. "Nothing to do except relax and read books while you lay in the sun and drink margaritas held to your lips by lithe and suntanned Cuban pool boys."

Mark looked sideward at his girlfriend as if she were crazy. "Where have you seen marketing like that?"

"In my mind," Inari said, twirling a lock of dark hair around her fingers.

"Yeah, I don't think pool boys hold the drinks up to your lips."

"I bet they would if you tipped them well enough."

Melody found their banter charming, and she would have enjoyed it if she weren't fretting over Larry's phone silence. She recognized that he was angry; it was stupid to have gotten in the car with Inari and Mark. She'd be stranded in Naples while Larry went home to Sunny. Alone.

"Hey, you okay back there?" Mark asked.

"I'm just worried," she said.

"You're hyperventilating. Call Larry and if he gets belligerent, I'll talk him down."

"That would be great," she lied, knowing full well she could never hand the phone off to anyone without facing Larry's wrath later.

When she heard Larry connect on the phone, but not say anything, she spoke first. "Larry, are you there?"

"Yes."

"Hey. I want to make sure you know where the Asian barbecue is so you find us easily."

"I don't want Chinese food," he hissed in her ear.

"Honey, they've got a sushi bar. You love sushi."

"Don't tell me what I love."

"Hey, I can give him directions!" Mark shouted from the driver's seat. He was intentionally loud and jovial.

"I'll find it," Larry said in her ear.

The call disconnected and Melody sat back a little more comfortably. At least she knew he wasn't on his way home without her. While the idea of having a meal with friends was pleasant, she wasn't willing to risk Sunny being alone with Larry.

"There's that bird store you get stuff for Sunny at," Inari said, pointing past Mark. "Do you wanna stop for anything?"

The huge word "pet birds" in orange letters was hard to miss among the store titles displayed for the little L-shaped strip mall. As a bird owner, Melody couldn't resist the call of a bird store. "Oh, yes. I need stuff."

Mark huffed a sort of laugh. "Girls and shopping."

"Shopping is a necessary art form after a solemn museum experience," Inari said. "That may have been important for my thesis, but it was harsh for my soul."

Mark was stopped at the light to hang a U-turn, nodding in agreement. "I get it. I saw that they offer tours for schools and stuff. Should be mandatory for school kids. Set it up on a rotation so that every damn junior high history class within a two- or three-hour drive goes through there every year for a reminder."

"So it can be harsh for a kid's soul?" Inari asked.

"Exactly. Kids are way too sheltered from reality. They need to know we once had a dictator in the world that convinced his soldiers to gas people because of their genes. Uncool."

"I'd like to hope we have enough science today to prove beyond a shadow of a doubt that we're all just men and women," Melody said. "No other differences. Just women. Just men. We don't need to gas one another over skin colors or the way we worship God."

"Amen," Inari muttered. "Give it to Your Bird? I remember that name now. Clever."

They had parked directly in front of the store they wanted, and Melody found herself excited. It was good to do something positive; getting a new toy for Sunny fit that definition perfectly. She could grab treat sticks for his travel cage, too.

Inside the store, she expected to see her friend who owned the place. Instead, a stranger stood behind the counter, looking a bit nervous at three customers walking in.

"Hi," Melody said. "Where's Genny?"

"She's at a Golden Retriever Rescue event today. They need to get some fosters set up with supplies before the storm. Can I help you with something?"

"Oh, no. I just need a toy for a sun conure."

"Pretty birds," the lady mused. "I love their colors." She watched Melody walk to the side of the store that had medium and large toys, and stopped making conversation.

Mark and Inari stayed on the side with an African grey parrot who had a sign about being adoptable. They had questions about that, which the lady was happy to answer. Melody was happy to pick through toys, looking for the ones with the best "chew factor" for Sunny.

52

When they got to the Zen Asian BBQ restaurant a couple blocks north of the store, Larry hadn't arrived yet.

"Do you think he's lost?" Mark asked.

"That's a possibility," Melody said. "But he may be delayed at the gas station."

"Or wrecking your car," Inari said.

"Not helpful," Mark sang into her hair. "You want me to stand out there on the sidewalk and wave him down?"

"In this heat?" Melody asked. "No, that's not necessary."

"He's likely to run you over," Inari said.

"Again, not helpful," Mark sang lowly, opening the restaurant door for the girls.

The waitress dressed in all black greeted them. "Three for dinner?"

"There might be four of us," Inari said. "But we'd like to be seated now."

"Sure. How about here by the window so you can see when your friend arrives?"

That sounded like a good idea.

"I'll bring four waters out, if you like," the woman offered, while placing the thick, bound menus on the table in front of each of them.

"Yes, please," Melody said.

"Could I also have a white Zin?" Inari asked.

"Do you have a favorite label?"

"Just the house will be fine."

The waitress nodded. "Anyone else need a cocktail or other drink to get started?"

Mark and Melody said no, and the wait for Larry began. At one point, Inari's cell phone beeped and she went out to the patio to talk to her father. Mark excused himself to stalk the front sidewalk in hopes of flagging down their lost companion. Melody put her elbow on the table and leaned her chin on the palm of her hand to stare at the five-foot waterfall against the wall. Water cascaded in a continual, calming flow over the peaceful face of Buddha with closed eyes while the overhead music played IZ's rendition of *Somewhere Over the Rainbow*.

The restaurant was named correctly. Zen. She could feel it offering a contrast to the unending jostling and bickering of expensive BMW, Lexus and Audis at the 7-11 across the street where moody octogenarians fueled up before the storm.

She looked back at the waterfall, and then down at the dark ceramic saucers on the table, their colors blending so harmoniously with the dark table top that a server somewhere behind her forgot them, and one clattered and shattered on the faux wood tile as the door in front of her opened, and Larry walked in. Mark followed.

"Look who I found," Mark announced, as if nothing odd had transpired in the parking lot.

Inari came in from the patio right behind them.

"Hey, Sweetie," Melody said. "You found us!"

"This place is kinda hidden," Larry complained as he took a seat next to her.

The four of them settled in as Inari said, "My dad is watching the weather channel and it looks like Bertha is moving toward North Carolina instead of here."

"We all lived through Charley," Larry said. "I wouldn't put a lot of stock in how the weathermen track these things."

Inari ignored him. "So instead of driving to Georgia tomorrow, I was thinking we could go to that farmer's market in Ft. Myers. I want to get peppers for the salsa Dad likes."

Mark made a yummy sound of approval. "I like it, Babe."

"Yeah, because it's easy to ignore the fate of people in North Carolina," Larry said.

"I can send them salsa," Inari snarked back.

"Funny," Larry said, pretending to smile.

"What are you guys doing tomorrow?" Mark asked.

"Haven't thought about it," Larry said. "But driving to Georgia wasn't in the plans."

"Well, not when one of your cars is undrivable. What happened there?" Inari prodded.

Melody squirmed in her seat, wishing Inari would stop antagonizing the man who was going to scream all the way home.

"A woman driver ran into me."

"Nice," Mark said. "You know, I've heard that distracted driving is on the rise despite it getting more attention than drunk driving campaigns. Was she on her cell phone?"

The three people at the table stared at Mark for a couple of seconds. While Melody wasn't certain which part of his statement would piss Larry off the most, she figured an explosion was imminent. She also thought she might have her mouth hanging open, so she picked up her water glass to cover that expression.

"I didn't notice a phone as I was distracted by her car ramming into mine."

"That makes sense," Mark conceded. "What did the cops say?"

"They gave us both tickets before escorting us to the hospital."

"You got a ticket from it?" Melody asked.

"Don't get pissy," Larry said. "I'll pay it."

"But you were hospitalized. Why would they add insult to injury and give you a ticket?" she asked. She didn't notice Inari frowning at her; she didn't realize she was "siding" with him.

"I don't know. Maybe to make the mom feel better about herself."

"She's a mom?" Inari asked. "How do you know?"

"Her kid was sitting right there. *That* was probably her distraction."

"Yeah, kids shouldn't be allowed in cars," Inari said sarcastically.

"Is the kid okay?" Melody asked. It bothered her that she hadn't thought to ask anything about the other car, the other vehicles' occupants, before. How could she have been conditioned inward?

"We'd have been told by now if he wasn't," Larry said, getting visibly uncomfortable.

"How old is he?" she asked.

"I don't know. Grade school? He was just a kid."

Mark was frowning at him. "There's one kid under the age of thirteen involved in a crash every thirty-three seconds. Congratulations on adding to the stats."

A couple trailing the waitress past the table glanced disapprovingly at the group.

"It wasn't my fault the lady had her kid loose in the car," Larry snarled. "And how do you know that stuff?"

Melody was remembering that Mark had some kind of government job.

"It's a common statistic from NHTSA," Mark provided. "That's the National Highway Traffic—"

"Whatever," Larry interrupted. "I was in the wrong intersection at the wrong time and a lady hit me. End of story."

"It's not just car accidents hurting kids," Mark said. "In our state alone, last year we had stats for, seventy-three kids under the age of five drowned."

"How do you know all this morbid stuff?" Larry asked.

"Then there are the kids who are hurt by alcoholic parents," Mark said.

The waitress walked by the table, returning menus to the stand by the front door, and Larry balled his hands into fists.

"Why did you get a table where every single person has to walk past us?" Larry asked.

"We're by the window—" Melody said.

"To look at the parked cars?" he interrupted. "Great view."

"To see when you arrived so we could—"

"So it's *my* fault that we're sitting where every single person has to walk past us and listen to our conversation. You're going to blame *me* for being in the highest trafficked spot in the restaurant."

Inari stopped Melody from responding. "Wow. You're able to be a martyr about everything, aren't you?"

"I'm not being a martyr," Larry snapped back. "I'm trying to understand why she's blaming *me* for her being a pushover. You know you can ask for a different table when a waiter offers you a bad one."

"I don't care where we're sitting, as long as the company is good," Mark said, holding up his glass as if in a toast.

Inari offered Larry a sideways smile as she lifted her glass to clink. "Hear, hear."

The waitress walked up to them with a genuine smile and asked if they were ready to order.

"I'm famished," Mark said.

"Do you have hamburgers?" Larry asked.

"Not really," she answered. "I can show you—" She reached for the menu in front of him, but he put his hand on it to stop her.

"I'm not really hungry," he interrupted. "I'll have a beer."

To her credit, the waitress smiled and spoke kindly to Larry, despite his tone with her. The rest of the meal seemed to move at a snail's pace to Melody. Each item in her Bento box was delicious, but each bite fell into her stomach like lead shot as she worried about the drive home and the night of anger she was to endure.

To her relief, Larry elected to drink so much Saki and beer that he slept all the way home. When she pulled the car into the garage, she couldn't wake him enough to get him out of the car. He rolled his eyes to look at her, but she could tell he wasn't seeing her. As she'd had to do in the past, she left him in the car, and went inside to wait for the rage.

Chapter 8

When Larry came in from the car, he stood in the kitchen for a few minutes, rubbing his face. She sat on the couch near Sunny's flight cage, reading *Choices Meant for Gods* from a local author with the stereo playing a Franz Ferdinand compact disc. All old school. All comforting.

She watched as Larry crossed the condo to the guest bathroom. Of course she noticed that he walked in a zig-zag pattern, holding onto furniture, exaggerating dizziness with a few steps here, standing perfectly upright there, stopping to burp once or twice. Was it an act, or was he too intoxicated to walk? The man drank enough vodka on a daily basis to keep Lee County's liquor industry in business, how did an evening of beer and a couple shots of Saki mess him up this much?

When she heard him vomiting in the bathroom, she remembered he had new medications that included Vicodin in his system. He had probably been administered morphine or Tramadol at the hospital overnight. There was no telling what kind of turmoil his body was in. She leaned her head back on the couch and closed her eyes. She prayed for strength and wisdom. What was she supposed to do to help him?

When he finally emerged from the bathroom, he crisscrossed the living room to his chair and dropped uneasily into it.

"Are you okay?" she asked.

He started to cry.

She wasn't confident enough in the situation to move yet. Staying on the couch, she asked, "What can I do?"

"I don't know," he sobbed. "I need help."

"Okay. You think on it, Sweetie. Tell me what to do when you're ready."

He nodded, still sobbing.

It broke her heart to see him crumpled like this. Even when she knew it was his fault for abusing his body, it hurt her to see him hurting. After a few minutes, she asked, "Are you still wearing the pain patch?"

He looked up at her, his head going through a circuitous route to face her. "What?"

"Do you still have the Fentanyl patch on?"

"I don't know...I don't know what...patch."

She nodded and set the book down on the couch. "Do you remember getting the pain patches at the pharmacy this morning?"

He nodded, but she didn't know if that was a true response or not.

"Do you remember putting one on after your shower?"

He shook his head this time, and then burped.

She walked over to put the small trashcan of pop tart wrappers and tissues from beside his chair on his lap. "Hold onto this in case you need it," she said.

"Where you going?" he slurred, suddenly panicked. "Don't leave me."

"I'm not leaving. I'm getting you a cool washcloth."

He nodded at that.

She went to the master bathroom to wet a washcloth for him, but she also looked in the trashcan, where she found the wrappers for two of the Fentanyl patches. She dug around the mess of his shaving utensils, hair products, books, and medicine bottles to see if anything else was amiss. No, the man was likely wearing both patches. The box had only one remaining.

When she took the washcloth out to him, she folded it over and placed it on the back of his neck. "Does that feel better?" she asked.

He nodded.

"Okay. I need you to take the pain patches off. You have two of them on, and they're hurting you."

He nodded, but the glassy look in his eyes told her he didn't comprehend her.

"Let's try it this way. Can you stand up?"

He nodded, but didn't move otherwise.

"Okay. Stand up for me?" She took the trashcan in one hand and his forearm in the other. "Ready?"

He understood then. Together, they got him standing upright.

"Hold the trashcan," she said.

He leaned slowly to the left while she lifted his shirt and searched his lower back and sides for the patches. Nothing.

"I'm going to lower your shorts so I can look for the patches, okay?"

He nodded.

"Try to stand up," she prodded, helping him to lean back toward center.

He leaned slowly to the right while she found a patch on his left hip.

"I don't know if you'll feel this or not," she said. "I'm gonna rip it off like a Band-Aid™, okay?"

That was easier said than done, but she got the sticky patch off his skin with minimal complaint from him. She placed it in the trashcan. The other patch was on his right hip; she repeated the process. With his shorts back in place, she helped him sit back down.

"Are you chilled?" she asked.

He shook his head.

"Okay. Do you need to lie down?"

He shook his head. "Don't let me die."

"You're not going to die."

58

"I need help. I need to go somewhere for help."

She sighed. They'd been through this scenario before. He'd been to clinics for detoxification before. Three-day detox was useless, and she knew it. But the idea of getting him out of the house for three days gave her such a sense of euphoria that she was willing to drive him to the nearest clinic and drop him off. The problem, of course, was finding the nearest clinic that had an open bed. It was almost midnight on a Saturday in Southwest Florida. The chances of finding an open bed in a detox facility were akin to winning the lottery.

She pulled out her cell phone and started with St. Matthew's House in Naples. They had his records on file. It would be easier for him if they could take him. She struck out with all the regional places. St. Matthew's, Hope House, Sovereign Health of Florida, and Mission Unity all turned them down, saying Larry had to be the one making the call, and then telling him nothing was available when she handed him the phone.

She finally found a center off Colonial Drive in Ft. Myers that indicated she could bring Larry that night, but she'd have to ring the front bell and wait for a tech to help her because the doors were locked after dusk. "No problem," she said. "I can be there in about twenty minutes."

She piled Larry into the passenger seat with the trashcan on his lap, reassuring him again and again that she wasn't leaving him. He fell asleep almost instantly and she thanked God for the reprieve in his worry. She had turned off the stereo to keep him calm and sat in utter silence at a red light, watching absolutely nothing go by. The night seemed to be at a standstill. The whir of the car's engine matched the whoosh of the air conditioning's fan. It was quiet until she heard trickling water.

"Great," she muttered, fearing the air conditioner might be malfunctioning. She was grateful for the silence that allowed her to hear the problem. Imagine if she'd had the stereo on and missed the first signs of the Oldsmobile falling apart.

Then she smelled something wrong. It was the smell of urine. She looked at Larry to see a growing patch of darkening fabric at his groin. He was still asleep, but the trickling sound continued while his shorts grew the dark patch of pee under the now-green glow from above.

She rolled the window down an inch to let the smell dissipate, and drove down the dark and deserted streets of Cape Coral toward Ft. Myers, toward a large stucco church, toward a dark and deserted brick building with locked glass doors. There were no other cars in the parking lot when she arrived, but most of the spots were marked for handicap-accessible vehicles. She parked as close to the door as she could, and hopped out quickly.

She pressed the clearly marked button next to the door and waited. And waited. And waited. And pressed the button again. And waited.

A lady's voice finally emanated from the speaker next to the button. "Can I help you?"

"My name is Melody. I spoke with someone about half an hour ago about bringing Lawrence Dos for the night."

"We got no beds tonight."

Click.

"What? Wait. I just spoke to someone."

There was no response.

"Hello?"

When she realized the person must have turned off the speaker, she pressed the button. Unceasingly.

This time a man wearing nice slacks, a button-down shirt, and a tie appeared behind the glass doors. "Ma'am? Could you stop? Ma'am?"

She let off the button when he opened the door to speak to her.

"I brought Lawrence Dos for help," she said. "He's in the car."

"Ma'am, we don't have any beds tonight, but you are welcome to call back to check availability—"

"No, I called," she interrupted. "I called and we both spoke to someone here. They told us to come. That was less than thirty minutes ago. He's right there in the car."

"I understand, but we don't have anywhere to put him. Have you tried Mission Unity?"

"Yes," she said, suppressing a sense of mania inside. "I've tried everywhere. You're the only place that has any beds. He needs help. He's wet himself and needs help."

"He urinated on himself?"

"Yes. On the way here. He's passed out."

"If he's suffering incontinence, that's a medical condition and we cannot admit him. You need to take him to the emergency room."

Melody stared at the man in shock. It occurred to her that she could roll Larry out of the car onto this man's feet, and then this medical professional that had once sworn to do no harm would have to help.

"Ma'am, are you okay?"

"What?"

"Are you crying?" he asked.

"No. No, I'm taking him to the emergency room."

She spun on her heel and marched back to the driver's side of the car.

"Drive safely," he called after her.

She didn't have the energy to respond.

When she got into the driver's seat, the smell of urine was present in the air again. She fought back tears as she pulled her seatbelt on and started the engine. "Okay," she said to herself. "Where's the hospital?"

She knew better than to take him to Cape Coral Hospital or Lee Memorial Hospital. Larry had large outstanding balances at those facilities; they would likely demand some kind of payment before treating him, and she had less than twenty dollars in her checking account at this point. His medications had taken an unexpected bite out of her budget. That left Gulf Coast Medical on Daniels Boulevard.

When she pulled up to the emergency room bay, she popped out of the car and got a wheelchair from just inside the doors. She locked its wheels in place outside of the car, piled Larry—wet shorts and all—into the chair, and placed the small trashcan on his lap. She unlocked the wheels and pushed him into the building, leaving him in the middle of the walkway while she parked the car. By the time she returned, someone had collected the comatose patient and the receptionist greeted her.

"Does he have insurance?"

"No."

"Does he have any allergies to medication?"

"No."

"Was he in an accident?"

"Friday afternoon."

The receptionist looked at her. "Are you okay, Ma'am?"

"I think I need to sit down. But I'm fine."

Chapter 9

Sunday morning broke while Melody drove them home. She couldn't believe the hospital wasn't keeping him. He didn't have the jaundiced look of impending death that he'd had seven hours before, but he surely wasn't sober yet. Whatever they'd given him had adsorbed some of the poison from his body, but he obviously still needed help getting in and out of the car.

At home, he wanted to get a shower and then get some sleep.

She was relieved by all of that. Her nerves were shot. She pulled out the vacuum cleaner and took advantage of his noise in the bathroom to get the vacuum noise out of the way. It was nice to get the floor cleaned without him complaining about it.

Then, when he turned the volume up on the television in the bedroom, she pulled her laptop out of its bag to do some work in the living room with Sunny. She had just sat down when Larry called her name.

Rather than yell, she got up and walked to the bedroom door. On the floor, next to the bed, the underwear and T-shirts she'd laundered Saturday morning were in a partially folded mass.

"What do you need?" she asked.

"Will you sit with me?"

"I'm going to let you get some sleep while I do some work," she said.

"You're disgusted by me, aren't you?" he asked.

"I'm not disgusted, Honey. I'm working. You're sleeping. That's all."

"You're going to leave me, aren't you?" he asked.

"I'm not leaving. I'm sitting on the couch with my computer."

"Okay," he pouted.

She closed the door to block some of the television noise.

* * *

By mid-afternoon, he wanted to get food. He got out of bed and moved his television viewing to the living room, announcing that he wanted to go out for an early dinner.

"Sweetie, I don't have any money for food," she said.

"How can that be? You're the one with the job."

She wasn't walking into that trap. Instead of answering his question, she asked, "How about I warm up some baked chicken? That should be easy on your stomach."

"I don't want leftovers. I want to go to Ruby Tuesday. I wanted to go there yesterday but your friends made us go to the Chinese food place. Let's go to Ruby Tuesday and have the salad bar. It'll be healthy."

"I can't do that today. We'll go after I get paid this week."

"I have money," he said.

"Money to waste on dining out?" she asked.

"Kev made the bike payment this week."

A few things suddenly made sense to her. His ability to put gas in his car and buy "coffee" and beer for the past few days fell into place. Kevin had come through.

Kevin was a fellow Larry had worked with at FedEx. The two of them acted like friends for a while. Kevin, being younger than Larry, had active weekends involving all-terrain vehicles, swamp buggies, speedboats on the Gulf, dirt bikes, and the expensive booze that playboys like. Kevin also had wealthy parents who lived in the area and enjoyed spoiling their adult son.

While he was still working at FedEx with Kevin, Larry had purchased a motorcycle that reminded him of one he'd owned—and lost in a confusing scenario to someone in North Carolina—over a decade earlier. The motorcycle was a hearkening to a wilder time, a freer time, a crazier time in his life. It had given him a sense of turning-back-the-clock to have the bike in the garage.

It also gave him a sense of mortality. Larry discovered that drivers had become more dangerous in the decade since his last two-wheeled dalliance with adventure. Larry found himself unwilling to risk life and limb around the elderly drivers of Southwest Florida, and sold the bike to Kevin. Kevin paid most of it immediately, but still owed Larry a couple hundred dollars. Melody stayed silent on the matter because Kevin's name sometimes sent Larry into fits of melancholy, sometimes into fits of rage.

"You want to spend your motorcycle money on dinner?" she asked.

"Come on. My treat. Let's go."

"Can I get cleaned up first?" she asked.

"You look fine. Let's go."

She should have stood her ground. Traffic was heavier than Larry wanted it to be. The waitress was slower than Larry wanted her to be. The salad bar wasn't stocked with the things Larry wanted to eat. His hamburger wasn't cooked to his liking.

He sent the hamburger back to be replaced, and Melody tried to ease the tension at their table. "It's good that you stood up for yourself," she said. "You deserve to get the hamburger you want."

He nodded. "Damn straight. I've been trying to tell Paula that."

"To stand up for herself?"

"No. That *I* stand up for *my*self. She's got all the confidence she needs. She needs to see that her old man does, too. All her life, she's seen me as the guy who had to get away from bad situations. I wasn't there for her because things went wrong for me. And I'm trying to make her see that I'm not a deadbeat. I'm a dad she can count on. I've got to get a new car."

The switch from "good dad" to "get a car" was not the jump in logic that an eavesdropper might think. Larry had decided to give his car to his only child for her high school graduation. Melody found that laudable. She also found it irresponsible; Larry would be left with no transportation. Since his accident Friday, he had no car to give Paula, and no transportation.

"Can you help me buy a car?" he asked.

"To give to Paula?"

"Not right away. I need a car to get to job interviews. There's no way I'm going to get a job without a car."

"It's something we'll have to work around," she said. "Let's see what the insurance company comes back with, okay? They may have the answer."

He nodded at that. "They better give me a new car," he said. "After all we pay in premiums, they owe me a car."

He seemed mollified by the idea of the insurance company taking care of his immediate transportation problem, but his attitude didn't improve overall. He thought it took longer to get home from the restaurant than it should have. To top the evening off, they both started to feel sickly within an hour of getting home.

"I think my stomach is still messed up from whatever happened to me last night," Larry announced over the theme song to C.O.P.S.

She was too nauseated to remind him that "whatever happened to him" was alcohol poisoning coupled with opiate abuse. Instead, she said, "I think your stomach is messed up from dinner. I don't feel well, either."

"Are you saying going to Ruby Tuesday was a mistake? I guess I can't make any right decisions, can I?"

She wasn't going to argue. She set her laptop to the side to search the master bathroom for medicine to settle her stomach.

"Do we have any Tums?" he called from the guest bathroom.

"Not in here," she said. "Do you have Pepto Bismol in there?"

"Nope. I guess you expect me to go buy those things since you're out of money."

She wasn't going to argue. She felt too sick.

"You know, if you didn't buy toys for that bird all the time, you'd have enough money to buy the things we need around here. I know you bought crap for that bird yesterday. There are humans in this house that need real supplies, real medicine."

She knelt beside the commode to vomit.

Within a few minutes, Larry was at the bathroom door. "If I give you some cash, will you get us some Pepto?" he asked.

She was still wiping her face when he switched on the bathroom fan to clear the smell.

"Will you?" he asked again. "I really feel sick and this stink is making it worse."

"No," she whispered. She took a washcloth with her as she pushed past him to go lie on the couch. She didn't even move the computer, merely closed the laptop and sprawled across it. It was warm under her belly. Sunny muttered at her, moving to the corner of his flight cage closest to her. His tiny little squeaks felt soothing. She didn't hear what Larry said from the bathroom; she just listened to Sunny's little squeaks of comfort.

Chapter 10

She thanked her lucky stars that food poisoning only lasts a few hours. When Monday morning dawned, she felt that she had a new outlook on life. She got ready for work, placed Sunny in his travel cage, and got all the way out of the driveway before she saw Larry appear in the front window with a look of confusion.

She waved goodbye as if it were perfectly normal for her to leave *after* the sun was up and without speaking to him. Her phone chimed in its cradle on the dash and she swiped it.

"Hi, Sweetie," she said.

"Where are you going?" Larry asked.

"To work. It's Monday."

"Aren't you sick?"

"Last night," she reminded him. "How are you feeling this morning?"

"Terrible. I need your car."

"Honey, I'll be home this evening. Do you need me to stop and pick something up on my way home?"

"No, I need your car," he groused. "Right now."

"I'm already running later than usual. I'm gonna get stuck in traffic on my way into Naples. Gimme a call later today and let me know what I can pick up for you, okay?"

"Fine."

He cut off the call, so she didn't have to. She also didn't have to guess what he needed her car for. He would be ripping the house apart looking for his hidden stashes of booze because he didn't have his car to go buy what he needed. As she understood it, the drugs from Saturday's expensive pharmacy run were supposed to control the cravings, so the need for the drink was psychosomatic at this point. She had no sympathy for him.

When she finally got to work, her email account was overwhelming, and included a few notes from Larry with subject lines that smacked of melodrama. She ignored those in favor of the work-related messages, until she saw one from the car insurance company with the words "Cancellation Notice" in the subject line. That got her immediate attention.

Reading the message, she quietly repeated "no, no, no" to herself. She grabbed her purse and took her insurance card out of her pocketbook. She called the customer service number and tapped her fingers on her desk while she listened to the menu options—none of which seemed a good category to select if calling in to panic. As luck would have it, she had the option of pressing "zero" to speak to a customer service representative.

A few minutes later, Melody read her policy number for the third time to the third customer service rep and waited as patiently as she could. Her blood pressure felt high.

"I have your information in front of me now, Ma'am. Could you verify your name for me again, please?"

"This is Melody Share. I need to find out why I received a cancellation notice this morning. I received an email from you all stating my policy is being terminated effective at midnight tonight. Is that legal? Can you do that? And why? What's going on?"

"Let me connect you to a supervisor."

She didn't get to respond to that, but was suddenly listening to the elevator treatment of *Stairway to Heaven*. She put a hand to her temple and imagined Robert Plant's voice in place of the jazzy clarinet.

When a supervisor finally joined her on the line, she was ready to burst into tears.

"Good morning. Could I have your policy number, please?"

"Omigod, I'm going to climb through this cell phone and start doing your job for you. I have already given my freaking policy number to three people. Now I want answers."

"I'm sorry for any inconvenience, Ma'am. If you could give *me* your number, I can pull your information up on my computer and help you."

"Okay," she said to calm herself. She provided the information the woman needed and listened to the clicking of computer keys.

"It appears a third incident occurred against your record Friday. When there are three incidents within a six-month period, policies are terminated. You'll see that in your—"

"Wait. A third incident? I haven't had any incidents. Lawrence Dos was involved in an accident, which was not his fault, but that's the only incident that could possibly be on my record. How is his incident affecting my insurance policy?"

"Miss Share, you and Mr. Dos have a joint policy for a Volvo S60 that was damaged Friday, is that correct?"

"Yes."

"Blame has been assigned to Mr. Dos for that incident, which resulted in multiple injuries. And I see that he received a speeding ticket while driving the Volvo the week prior. He also received a D.U.I. while driving the Volvo in Georgia in April. In fact, the policy should have been revoked at that time. We have a zero tolerance for alcohol-related incidents. Could you hold, please?"

Melody felt her head spinning. For a moment, she wondered which was going to be worse, confronting Larry about hiding a D.U.I. and speeding ticket, or telling him she wasn't going to share insurance expenses with him any longer. She looked at Sunny sitting calmly on his perch in the travel cage and said, "Sweetie, this is coming to a head."

* * *

"Well, look who's in my garage!" Betty said. "I'm kinda busy working right now, Mels."

While her words sounded like contradictions, they weren't. Betty actually worked in a garage that had been almost converted into an office. It was no secret that CRaP LLC was expanding in manpower faster than it was expanding in buildings, so a dozen people were crammed in two trailers on one side of the street, and Betty was crammed in the back of the one-car garage of the directors' building. In the front of the garage stood an impressive maze of file cabinets.

"I need a lawyer," Melody said.

"Don't you have a good lawyer who helped you with your divorce? Hold on a minute." Betty picked up her office phone's handset and used her smart phone stylus to punch buttons. After a couple seconds, she spoke into the receiver. "Hey, Monique. It's Bets. Did you forward the Ecumenny textbook file to Dr. Mason?"

Pause.

"Got it. Will you send that message to me, too? Thanks, Mone."

She put the handset back down and returned to her computer while she spoke to Melody. "Your divorce attorney was an awesome guy."

"Yes. But now I need someone cutthroat and horrible."

Betty looked over her shoulder at Melody and offered a sideward smile. "Mmm. I'm intrigued. Step into my garage. But gimme just a second."

Melody sighed as she took a seat in one of the company's ubiquitous white lawn chairs. Betty's affectations were tiresome, at best, but she had a certain set of friends outside of work—friends Melody needed access to. And the best way to get past Betty's affectations was to stroke the woman's ego.

"Wow, you *are* busy," Melody said, as if impressed. "What's the Ecumenny text? Something big?"

Betty closed whatever window had been open on her computer screen and swiveled her chair to face Melody. "Something ginormous." Betty emphasized the word with jazz hands and wide eyes. "It's the *Studies in Ecumenical Catholic Texts* for Mr. Dokins. It's going to be huge when it's done and I'm the lead on the project."

"So...its acronym is sect?"

"What?" Betsy asked, as if wanting an answer.

"Never mind. I think it's a great opportunity. That's the sort of project that might finally get you out of this garage."

"That. I'm getting out of here this week. I found a dead lizard and took it to Dr. Mason. I just couldn't stand it anymore. I mean, dead reptiles. In my office. I dropped it right on her desk. I finally broke down. I cried until she promised to fix it. Ken's moving in here. I get his office. Ken's. Office."

Melody refrained from suggesting that crying until you get your way might not be the type of behavior the original feminists had in mind for this generation. She was on a mission for specific information and needed to get Betty back on track.

"It'll be good to have Ken out of the trailer," Melody said.

"Well, I don't care what they do with Ken. He's a nice enough guy."

"I've yet to have a conversation with him where I feel comfortable," Melody said.

"Ken Doll? He's harmless!"

"He's a pig. But he's not the one I need to sue. I need your help."

"You need to sue someone?" Betty's voice turned conspiratorial.

"I need to sue my car insurance company."

Betty's mouth popped open with an actual pop sound. "Whaaa? You go, girl. Dish. Tell me everything."

"Larry was in a car accident Friday afternoon, which he would not have been in if the insurance company had done their due diligence and cancelled our policy back in April. The insurance company has put him, me, the entire motoring public in danger for two months."

Betty blinked her eyes and shook her head rapidly. "I don't get it. And when did you get so bitchy?"

"I don't really believe all this crap. Larry is responsible for his own actions. But I know that a cutthroat attorney can prove it. If the insurance company had alerted me to what was going on behind my back, if they had cancelled my policy in accordance with their own rules in April of this year, if they had performed their due diligence even two weeks ago, Larry would not have been on the roads endangering anyone and would not have caused an accident Friday."

"In accordance with their own rules? Due diligence? Gawd, Mels. You sound like your own cutthroat attorney."

"But I'm not. People who pretend to be attorneys when they're not can get in lots of trouble. So I need you to get me in touch with a real one. One who would like to make a lot of money off of my insurance company's gross incompetence."

Betty stared at her for a minute. Then she smiled and purred like a sadist, "Mels, I don't *ever* want to make you mad."

Chapter 11

With Betty getting an attorney lined up for her, Melody used her meager emergency bank account to set up a new car policy with The General Insurance Company. It was frighteningly expensive, but the best she could come up with on short notice. She insured only her Oldsmobile and only herself. That would be an argument with Larry later, but trying to insure him would have been next to impossible.

She had barely resolved the insurance problem before her office phone rang with a call from Gulf Coast Medical in Ft. Myers. The woman on the line introduced herself, but all Melody heard was the name of the facility.

"Oh, no. Is Larry there again? Is he okay? What happened?"

"No, Ma'am. I'm in the accounting department. I'm calling with questions about Mr. Dos's bill."

Melody relaxed. "Thank goodness. I was afraid he'd hurt himself at the house or something. How can I help?"

"Well, it appears he has no health insurance and he's not on Medicaid. Is that correct?"

Melody felt a tingle at the back of her neck. She needed to be careful.

"I'm not sure if he has Medicaid, but I know he doesn't have health insurance. He hasn't been able to pay me any rent for a few months now, and I think he lost his health insurance when he lost his job."

"I beg your pardon?" the accountant asked.

"He lost his job a few months back, and he's running up quite a tab for the room." Melody felt her self-respect slipping. The ruse of Larry being "just a roommate" was easier to perpetrate now that she and Larry constantly fought and didn't share intimate contact. But it still felt like a boldface lie to tell billing departments and creditors that Larry was not dependent on her.

"Does Mr. Dos pay rent to live at 1494 Northwest 5th Street?"

"Not lately," Melody laughed. "But I'm sure he'll get back on his feet soon."

"So your salary isn't a factor in his income?" the woman asked.

"Oh, no. My salary is my own. His salary, when he gets back to making one, will be his own. Did you already speak to him about this? I'm not sure if I'm legally allowed to discuss his finances, since he's kind of a tenant."

"He listed you as his fiancé on his emergency room—"

"Fiancé?" Melody blurted out. "Holy cow, no. We are *not* engaged. He was under the influence of a lot of medication when I helped him to the E.R. the other night. Does the form say what they treated him for? That might explain his confusion."

"Yessss," the woman answered. "Could I ask you to have Mr. Dos submit an itemized list of expenses to our accounting department? We will need to evaluate income versus expenses to prepare his bill."

"I'll let him know to call you," Melody said.

After some niceties, they ended the call, and Melody sat with her head in her hands for a few minutes. The last thing she wanted to do was broach the topic of expenses with Larry. Again. A list of them? That was asking for trouble. Again.

Chapter 12

She couldn't wake him. He was breathing, so she knew he was alive. She went back out to the kitchen where Sunny waited in his travel cage. The bird looked up at her as she approached. "I guess we wait for that argument," she told him. "Would you like some little green trees?"

Sunny squeaked. The smart bird knew that meant broccoli, which was fantastic. She put him in his flight cage with some broccoli florets and sat down to do some work on the computer while she waited for Larry to wake. While sitting on the couch, she realized the den had a new sound. Something in the den was chirping, and that made no sense to her. As she moved toward the room to investigate, she noticed a warm humidity to the air.

When she stepped into the room, she immediately saw the window was open. Not only open, but missing its screen. She glanced around the room, taking a quick inventory to ensure the computer, printer, shredder, backup drive, modem, CD player, fire-proof safe, all the things easy to carry away and sell were still in place. It made no sense that someone would break in and take none of these easy things from the room.

She crossed to the window and looked out to see if the screen was outside. It was. In fact, it appeared to have fallen against an egg crate full of plastic vodka bottles behind the bushes. Easily within arm's reach.

She put both hands on the sill and leaned there for a minute, her head hanging down. She closed her eyes and listened to a bird chirping in the bushes. It occurred to her that the bird in the bushes was telling her all his tales, singing his heart out, unburdening himself of the secrets he had been keeping regarding the stash of bottles hidden under an unlocked window. In the living room behind her, Sunny squawked as if in answer. It was his distress call; she'd been out of sight in this disturbing room too long.

She didn't bother reaching for the screen. She merely closed and locked the window. When she stepped into the living room, she stopped in her tracks and felt her blood turn cold and sluggish in her veins.

Larry sat in his chair with Sunny encircled in one hand. He held her precious bird around the neck to avoid being bitten by the strong and angry beak. Sunny wasn't struggling, but stared straight back at Melody. The bird's dark brown eyes were as wide as the white skin around them. He didn't even squeak. He just stared back at Melody, quietly staring. Quietly blinking. Quietly breathing in rapid, bird breaths.

Larry had his pistol in the other hand.

"What are you doing?" she asked quietly.

"I could ask you the same thing."

They were speaking to one another in the deep tones of people who met in dark alleyways—untrusting. Uncertain. Measured.

"I closed the window in the den," she answered.

"This obnoxious little shit bit me."

"He's not used to being held like that," she said. It felt as if she was swallowing her heart to keep it in her chest. "You probably scared him."

"You know..." Larry shook the gun, and Melody could see that his finger was inside the trigger guard. He wasn't pointing it at Sunny, but he was shaking it around randomly. "You're so lucky you get to live here." He was talking to Sunny now. "You have no idea how lucky you are that I let you live here."

"Larry," she marched across the room and reached for his hand. "Give him to me."

She didn't give him a choice. She put one hand under Sunny's feet and put her other hand on Larry's wrist. He instinctively released the bird, who flew with a squawk up to her chest. A few of his tail feathers dropped, fluttering, flittering to the floor from the stress. She stepped away, covering Sunny with her hands as she went to the master bathroom with him. She had to check him for injury. She had to make sure Larry hadn't broken any of his fragile bones.

"That bird's just lucky I let him live here," Larry yelled after her.

* * *

She stayed in the bathroom with the door locked most of the night. At one point, she crept out to gather Sunny's travel cage and her change of clothes for the morning. Then she was back to the safety of the little room with her tiny feathered friend she was responsible for protecting.

As she carried Sunny to the car Tuesday morning, she stopped at Larry's chair. He stared at her with a maniacal sort of glare.

"You can't live in the bathroom," he said. "When you get home tonight, we have to talk."

"I needed to discuss a couple things with you last night. Where's your gun?"

"I'm not going to shoot you," he snarled.

"Where is it?" she repeated.

"I put it back in the nightstand. Where it always is. Where I can protect this house."

She nodded as if accepting what he said. "All right. Now, listen carefully. I received an email—"

74

"Don't act like you're giving me an ultimatum," he said. "It makes you sound crazy. We can talk when you get home."

She ignored his interruption and continued. "I received an email from the insurance company yesterday. They have canceled our car policy as of midnight last night."

"What? Why didn't you tell me—"

"I was going to tell you before you started waving a gun around. Now, listen. You are no longer insured. I suggest you don't drive around in anyone's car until you fix that. Next. I also got a call from the hospital. The Gulf Coast hospital you were at Sunday morning. They need evidence to prove you can't pay big medical expenses or else they're going to send you a huge bill. You have to prove to them that you have half of the expenses here. Do you understand that?"

He nodded.

"I told them that you would call them," she continued. "Will you do that, or do you need me to send you an email to remind you?"

"I'm not a child."

"All right," she said. "I'm going to work."

"You're not going to stay here and talk about what happened?" he asked.

"No. I'm going to work and we can solve things when I get back this evening." She wasn't about to suggest that she was going to look for a new place to live on her way back. The days for resolution were over. He had crossed the line.

"How am I supposed to tell the hospital what my expenses are?" he asked.

"You can dig the list I gave you last week out of the trash."

"Oh, that's real mature," he said. "You're bringing up my invoice again?"

"I'm merely pointing out how much easier it would be for you if you hadn't acted like a fool last week when we were talking about fiduciary matters—"

"Fidushy what? Who do you think you are? You think this is all my fault. You think it's *my* fault that I need to come up with numbers for a hospital when you're the one who won't help me."

"Larry, I'm tired of doing the same things over and over again. Now, I'm going to work."

"If you think I'm coming up with money for your invoice today, I'll be gone when you get home," he called after her.

She'd heard that before, and found it comforting. Again.

She buckled Sunny's travel cage into the passenger seat and was about to back out of the garage when Larry walked out to berate her some more. She shook her head, wondering if the neighbors ever saw him running around in his boxers in the early morning. Rather than waiting for him to get mad about the glass between them, she rolled the window down just a couple of inches. She'd learned her lesson last week, though, and didn't open the window enough to let him get his hand in this time.

"Do you have the list?" he asked.

"I have a copy saved on my computer."

"Of course you do," he said. "I knew it. I knew you were keeping a tally. You expect me to pay you to live here, don't you?"

"No," she said. "I suspected you would lose track of the paper because you can't even keep track of your pants, so I saved a copy of the list on my computer to make it easier—"

"Whatever. Will you send it to me?"

"Yes."

"And who am I giving it to?" he asked.

"Gulf Coast Medical. I'll also send you the name of the accounting person who called me, okay?"

"Don't treat me like a child," he said. "I'm willing to lie to the hospital for you, but I'm not paying you thousands of dollars for living here, making your meals, cleaning your house, protecting you, taking care of you. I'm not your sugar daddy and I'm not going to be here tonight if you think I have to pay up after all I've done for you."

She swallowed the angry words she wanted to say, and instead said, "I certainly wouldn't expect you to stay with someone who takes advantage of you like that."

Chapter 13

During her drive to work, Melody left a voice mail message for the proprietor of Give it to Your Bird. She needed a place for Sunny to stay where he would be safe. Then she placed a call that her pride had prevented her from making for far too long. While at a red light, she pressed the buttons on her phone for Julia Christian.

"You're calling really early," Julia said in greeting.

"I know. I'm sorry. I know it's only six in the morning there."

"Yeah, but I was awake. I'm sitting here in my summer pajamas thinking about doing nothing all day. It'll be great!"

Melody could picture it. Her best friend lived in the Midwest, so Melody didn't see her very often, but she knew her blond wavy hair was cut in a short, cute crop this summer. She knew Julia preferred long sleep shirts for pajamas, so she knew she'd be curled up on the couch in something made of cotton with a blue Tardis pattern on it.

"You're going to work, right?" Julia asked.

"Yes. Yes, I am."

"Sucker. The best three things about being a teacher are June, July, and August."

"Don't forget spring break," Melody added. Summer break and early morning meant Julia would also be wearing her glasses, probably holding a glass of iced Coca Cola.

"Yep. Why are you calling this early? What's wrong?"

"You know me well."

"Yeah. What's wrong?" Julia asked again.

"Larry has gone off his rocker."

"Again," Julia said. It was a statement of fact, not a question.

"Fully. I have to get away from him before something really bad happens."

"Do you hear this?" Julia asked.

"What?"

"That's the sound of the zipper on my suitcase. Can you pick me up from the airport if I fly down there today?"

Melody almost burst into tears. It took a second to compose herself before she could speak.

"Mel?" Julia asked. "Are you still there?"

"Yes. Yes...just...I don't think today is great timing. I think I need to get a restraining order. I don't know what I need."

"You need me down there while you kick this guy's ass. Where's Sunny?"

At the sound of his name, Sunny gave a squawk.

"He's in his travel cage next to me."

"Good. You don't need to be worried about Larry doing something stupid to Sunny."

Melody felt the urge to cry rising up in her again. How had she let things get this bad?

"Are you staying at a hotel?" Julia asked.

"Oh, no. I don't have the funds for that. I had to tap into my emergency stash to deal with car insurance yesterday. A lot's been going on."

"Sounds like it. Why haven't you called me before now?"

"It was a crammed weekend," Melody said.

"I'll accept that for the moment. You go to work. I'll look at flights. We'll connect later today. How does that sound?"

"That sounds awesome."

* * *

By mid-afternoon, Melody wished she had encouraged Julia to fly on down to Florida that day. The number of roadblocks forming in her path to moving away from Larry seemed supernatural. It began with a call to the landlord, a Ms. Nellie Tarnet who represented the owner of the condo where she and Larry were both listed on a twelve-month lease. When Melody identified herself, the landlord didn't recognize who she was.

"I'm one of the tenants at 1494 Northwest 5th Street in Cape Coral."

"Oh," the woman said, giving the word a full octave drop. "Is this about the water again? Because if I send a worker out there and it turns out to be ants in the box outside, after the last worker showed you how to solve the problem, you will get charged for the service call."

"No, no, the water is fine—"

"Because pest control is your responsibility," Ms. Tarnet continued. "The utility areas must be protected from pest infestation as well as the house and grounds. You will be charged for any damage to the utilities if it's a problem caused by pests."

"There's nothing wrong with the utilities," Melody snapped. "I have a problem with the other tenant waving a gun in my face." She realized the woman on the other end of the phone wasn't going to care if Larry had waved a gun at a pet. Because Melody had been in the same room, she felt comfortable with the exaggeration.

The landlord was silent for a moment, and then said, "I see. There aren't supposed to be any weapons on the property."

"Yeah, well, that's another problem we have, then." Melody felt her patience growing thin.

Melody asked question after question about having Larry removed from the property. The landlord responded with the same basic line of uselessness.

"I can't legally remove his name from the lease without serving an eviction notice," Ms. Tarnet cooed. "And that is a very involved process that takes time and costs fees through the courthouse."

"Okay," Melody said. She recognized her overuse of the word lately. It served as some kind of coping mechanism to use the word to calm her, to buy a minute to think. "So how can we protect me? How can we get *him* off the property?"

"You really can't," the woman told her. "You'd have to get a restraining order against him, but no judge is going to prevent a person from entering his own home."

"Right. So that's where you have to help me. I'm willing to leave so that no one is preventing him from entering his home. Can you rewrite the lease so I'm not on it? Don't evict me; just let me leave so I don't end up shot in the head, which will leave quite a mess on the property."

The woman made a clucking sound. "I'm so so sorry. But no. You're the one who has the income to pay the rent, so you're the one my client will want on the lease. Lawrence is of no value. If you leave, you're breaking the lease, and you don't want *that* on your record."

"I can tell you right now, Ms. Tarnet, I'd rather a broken lease than a broken neck."

Melody had decided even before her call to Ms. Tarnet that she'd need a restraining order against Larry, but that would have to wait for another day. Her next roadblock came from out of left field.

She had contacted an older friend of Betty's upon reaching the office that morning. The friend had a furnished apartment for rent still in Lee County, but closer to work and for less cash per month than the condo, and in an area full of security cameras. Melody didn't even need to see it. She was ready to move in. She sent the information that Ms. Genie Dirvish requested that morning, and was initially pleased to get a call back from the potential new landlord that afternoon.

"Ms. Share, I received your background check and credit report."

"Great!" Melody said. "Betty said you need a money order for the security deposit on the place. I can bring that to you on my way home from work if that's okay. It'll be later in the evening."

"Ms. Share, there's a problem."

"There's what?"

"You've run up a lot of charges out of Chicago. How do you intend to make your rent payment each month with this kind of debt load? I know Betty thinks you're capable, but this looks overwhelming to me, and I'm an excellent accountant. I understand numbers and cash flow very well."

Melody was silent for a moment, letting the sentences seep into her brain. Charges out of Chicago? That made no sense.

"Ms. Share? Are you still on the phone?"

"Yes. Yes, I'm here. But I don't understand. I don't have any business in Chicago. What charges are you talking about?"

"Your new X5 is from Perillo BMW. Your furniture, which won't fit in this efficiency apartment, is from Ashley HomeStore in Burbank. Are you also going to rent a storage unit for your expensive belongings? Your—"

"Oh no. Stop," Melody interrupted her. "Are you looking at *my* credit report? The report for Melody Share? Not someone else from Catholic Research and Publishing LLC?"

"I don't appreciate you calling my records into question," Ms. Dirvish said. "I keep excellent records. And this credit report reads like a person who has no self control and does not keep good records at all."

"Ms. Dirvish, I think I know what's happened. Please let me explain. One of my co-workers told me, just last week, that her identity had been stolen. All the charges were out of Chicago. They caught it when someone tried to open a Wal-Mart credit card in her name. Is there a Wal-Mart charge card on my report? A Wal-Mart in the Chicago area?"

"Let me look."

It was the longest two minutes of her life.

"Yes. Niles, Illinois."

"Ms. Dirvish, I've not been to Chicago for years. Years, I tell you. And I have no reason to open a Wal-Mart account up there when I live down here. Someone has stolen my co-worker's identity and apparently mine. And this makes me think I need to contact H.R. to make them aware of it. I mean, what are the chances of this happening to two people in the same building? Look…I can make the rent payments. You can count on me. Can I bring you the security deposit tonight, after 6:00 or 7:00?"

There was a pause.

"Yes. That'll be fine."

"Oh, thank you. I'll figure out how to get there from Betty."

She saw her cell phone light up while she was hanging up with the new landlord.

"Hello?"

"Hi, Melody. This is Genny. You needed something for Sunny?"

"Yes! Thank you for calling me back. I've got to get him somewhere safe tonight. Can you board him for a few days?"

"I'm packed here, but Wendy may have room."

They were talking about arrangements for Sunny when Dr. Mason appeared in Melody's doorway.

* * *

Dr. Mason was not a young woman. She'd seen many years as a stay-at-home mom before going back to school for her masters in business management. While laudable, the feat was tainted by her doctorate diploma coming from a questionable online university that had lost its bid for accreditation the first year its millionaire chancellor had applied for it.

Somehow, the officials at CRaP LLC collected Karla Mason from her position in insurance sales and put her in charge of managing incoming projects for a publishing house. No one who worked for her could figure out what qualified her for a job of organizing projects that salespeople brought in, but no one questioned it for long. Her department had the highest turnover rate in the entire company.

She stood in Melody's doorway until the conversation about where to take Sunny finished, and then stepped in, offering a tight, polite smile with wrinkled lips. She had reached that age and stage where lipstick strayed up and down the wrinkles, giving her mouth a jagged look.

"Please have a seat, Dr. Mason," Melody invited her as calmly as possible. "Thank you for your patience while I finished that up."

The woman gestured toward the travel cage. Sunny wiggled his long green and blue-tinged tail feathers as he ducked into his cozy cave. "And how is the little bird?"

Melody recognized the hint of danger in the tone of her boss's voice, and decided to answer with shock and awe.

"He's going to be okay. We had a big fright last night when Larry pulled a gun on him."

Dr. Mason had the decency to be genuinely aghast. She put both of her hands in her lap demurely as she sat in the lawn chair. "Melody, are you safe?"

"I will be. I'm taking Sunny to a friend on my way home. I've been advised to get a restraining order against Larry. This nightmare will be over soon."

Dr. Mason stared at her for a moment, processing this new information. She appeared to be struggling with a new battle strategy. Melody did nothing to interrupt, but quietly waited, considering her own options. As if anticipating chess moves, she visualized what to do if Dr. Mason suggested Melody take on more work to keep her mind off her problems at home.

"I see," the older woman finally said. "I was very concerned about your safety. And your work. It's hard to do your job effectively when afraid for…for one's safety. Do you need some time off of work?"

"I'm safer here," Melody said. "But you're so kind to worry for me. Thank you."

"Of course. It really touched me when I heard that you were no longer engaged to Larry, that the two of you weren't getting married. It touched me." The woman put her aged and dry hand to her chest, over her heart, as if indicating her heart was in any way moved by anything.

"It was a decision I *had* to make," Melody said, as if admitting the two has ever been engaged. As if admitting a deep secret.

She'd worked in the company for several years; she knew how this game was played. "May I share something with you? Something emotional?"

Dr. Mason leaned forward in the chair. She actually licked her lips. "Of course."

"I loved Larry deeply at one time," Melody said. While true, the words tasted like dirt in her mouth. She spewed the uber-Catholic rhetoric the boss needed to hear. She lowered her voice to say, "It's difficult to admit that my love and trust were misplaced. I was raised to only marry someone you truly love, and I thought that was going to come true with Larry. It breaks my heart to know I was duped."

Dr. Mason nodded. "I understand. If you need someone to talk to, my door will be open. If you need to take a vacation day to deal with any of this, just file the form with Mr. Marx. You have my permission."

"I might go see him next," Melody said, as if Dr. Mason had put the idea in her head. "You're very wise."

"That's great," Dr. Mason affirmed through her wrinkly smile. "That's great."

Melody waited several minutes after Dr. Mason had stalked out on her stiletto heels before breathing normally again. Most people didn't get a visit from that particular director unless Secretary Avito followed the visit with a pink slip and a member of security escorting the person off the property. The last thing Melody needed at that moment was to get fired. She was about to use the last five hundred dollars of her emergency funds to pay a security deposit for a three-hundred-square-foot efficiency apartment that might or might not have a heating unit in it. There'd be nothing left to live on if the next day's paycheck didn't clear.

With her heart rate returned to normal, Melody told Sunny to be a good bird while she went to visit human resources, and she stepped outside the trailer.

"Hey, Melody!" Ken Bilso called.

"Seriously," she muttered. She wondered if the man stalked her, or if she truly had the bad luck of catching him on his smoke break all the time.

"Hi, Ken," she called back, not stopping.

"Wait up!"

"I've got to get to H.R.," she said, still not stopping.

"But wait!" he called again, jogging toward her. "What did Doc Mason want? Spill the beans, girl."

She couldn't keep walking without appearing rude, so she stopped. "Oh, she was just being supportive. Really nice," Melody lied with finesse. "Really nice of her."

"Supportive? What's up?" he pried.

"I'm just going through some stuff. It's gonna be fine. She was really nice to show how much she cares."

He wrinkled up his nose to laugh. "Riiiiiight."

She lost track of the syllables he inserted in the word. Did they both know they were lying to each other?

"What's really going on?" he asked. "I hear she's moving my office into the garage with Betty. That'll be a laugh-a-minute. Not! Hey, I've got a joke for you."

"I've really got to get going, Ken."

"What's the difference between peanut butter and jam?" he asked, tilting his head from left to right and back again.

"I don't want to know. I've got to get over to H.R. before—"

"I can't peanut butter my dick up your ass! Ha!" He hunched his shoulders up and forward as he started his rasping laugh. She thought she saw actual phlegm pop out of his mouth.

"That's horrible," she said, turning away from him. "Don't tell anyone else that joke."

"You got it, girl. It's our private joke!"

"It's nobody's joke, Ken. It's gross."

She was still snarling inwardly when she got to Mr. Marx's office. The secretary there blocked her path.

"You don't have an appointment, Ms. Share."

"I'm aware of that, but I do have an identity theft problem linked directly to this publishing house."

The woman scoffed. "I don't see how that's Mr. Marx's business."

"The news station might," Melody bluffed.

"I beg your pardon?"

"A news station in Chicago, specifically."

The woman frowned, as if trying to judge the sincerity of Melody's comment.

"I also need to file a sexual harassment complaint against Ken Bilso. The sooner I do that, the better."

"Have a seat," the secretary said. She ducked into Mr. Marx's office.

Melody could only imagine the conversation that took place. *"Melody Share is threatening us." "With what?" "Exposure and sexual harassment."*

Trying to stay employed suddenly felt difficult.

"Ms. Share? Mr. Marx will see you now."

Chapter 14

She found the tiny apartment hardly worth four hundred dollars a month, but the landlord already knew she was in dire straights. She would be paying $1.67 per square foot to live at the back of the detached garage of a sketchy duplex. She'd be parking her car on the low end of a flood zone. The unkempt woman renting the apartment to her came to the front door of the duplex in a pale muumuu that didn't really hide the fact that she was naked beneath it. The woman smelled of bad seafood.

But the apartment was reasonably clean, the furniture was only slightly mildewed, and the coin Laundromat was only three blocks down the street. She could move in that weekend. She handed the security deposit to Ms. Dirvish, signed the lease agreement, and took Sunny to her friend Wendy's house for the rest of the week. They settled him into a nice-sized cage with his own toys and sleeping cave to make it feel less foreign.

"Are you gonna be okay?" Wendy asked her.

"I'm gonna miss this little guy until Saturday. Make sure he gets all the treats he wants," she handed Wendy a bag of said treats. "He's used to being at my side all the time. He'll need lots of attention."

Wendy winked at her. "Don't worry about a thing. I'll keep him spoiled until Saturday."

"I can't pay you until I pick him up. My account is drained today."

"Girlfriend, you won't pay me then, either. This is the least I can do after what Genny said you're going through. If you need me to help kick that guy's ass, you let me know."

Melody wondered why she hadn't asked for help before. While a number of her friends had taken the easy road of avoidance when it came to dealing with "the Larry factor," there were other friends like Julia—and now Wendy—who would be happy to step in and make sure she didn't get killed. Why hadn't she called on them before conditions eroded to this level? It was startling to think she had been desensitized to abusive behavior. She'd been desensitized until she was in need of a restraining order to keep a man from harming her when she tried to get away from him.

* * *

During her drive home, Melody's cell phone chimed its "unknown caller" sound. Because she sat at a red light staring at another car's brake lights, she reached forward and swiped "answer" where the phone sat cradled on the dash.

"May I speak with Ms. Melody Share?"

The gentleman's official sounding voice struck a nerve. Something was wrong. This wasn't a courtesy call from an officer at a hospital. Melody sat up a little straighter in the driver's seat.

"This is she."

"Ma'am, do you know a Mr. Lawrence Schmell Dos?"

Her heart rate quickened as the first scenario flashed across the screen in her mind. She pictured Larry lying on the driveway, broken from falling off the roof trying to chase away phantoms and specters.

"Umm, yes, I know him," she said. A part of her wanted to pick up the smart phone and hold it to her ear. The emotions evoked by the severity of the man's voice made her want to bring the conversation closer to her body, make it less open than talking into the air of the car's cabin.

"Ma'am, this is Deputy Sheriff Carlos Rodriguez. Do you live at 1494 Northwest 5th Street with Mr. Dos?"

Another scenario hit her brain. She saw Larry with his bloodied arm draped over the side of the guest bathroom tub, a razor blade dropped from his shaking fingers. There was no doubt in her mind he would use a knife or pills to kill himself if he went through with something so horrible. He wouldn't use his gun; that was reserved for threatening her and Sunny. For some stupid reason, tears welled up in her eyes as she answered, "Yes, I live there with Larry."

"Ma'am, are there any weapons in the house?"

"Omigod. Is he okay? Did he hurt himself?"

A loud honk jarred her from the worry. She had to drive.

"Ma'am, do you have reason to believe Mr. Dos would hurt himself?"

"What? There are a lot of reasons, but I don't understand. Yes, there's a gun; Larry owns a gun, but it's in the bedroom. In the nightstand. Is he okay?"

"Do you know if the gun is loaded?"

"Yes, yes, he keeps it loaded. Is he okay?"

"Mr. Dos is all right," the officer finally told her. "He asked us to contact you. He's concerned about you."

"Me? I'm on my way home right now. I can be there in like ten minutes. Maybe fifteen; there's traffic."

"Drive safely, Ma'am. We'll be here with him. He's concerned for your safety and wanted to make sure you were on your way home."

"What? Why didn't he call me? You know, never mind that. It's okay. I'll be there in a few minutes."

"Thank you, Ma'am. Drive safely."

She reached forward to swipe the "disconnect" feature on the phone and spent the next fifteen minutes in emotional turmoil. She swung from worry to anger to apathy to concern to frustration. Like her drive to and from Naples every day, she was back and forth between caring and not caring what happened to this annoying man.

Why on earth would he call the police to have the police call her? It made no sense. But then, why would the police decide to go to the house and hang out with him and then make the phone call? What was going on at her home?

When she got to the front gate at the community, the judgmental gaze of the guard met her first. Apparently, "much" was going on at her home.

She turned the corner onto Northwest 5th Street to see a fire truck, an ambulance, three police cruisers, and one of those deep burgundy unmarked Chevrolet Chargers the Cape Coral Police Department had purchased a few years back. Surprised to see one still in employ, she muttered to herself, "I thought Naples took all Lee County's hand-me-downs."

She recognized her snide remark as a coping mechanism. The sight of all the emergency personnel clogging the narrow street pulled the knot in her stomach tighter. "I'm gonna barf," she told the passenger seat, before realizing the travel cage didn't have Sunny in it. Her heart sank as she slowed the car into the driveway alongside a cruiser. "Don't even have my sweet little dude to help me through this."

An officer nodded as she walked toward the front door. Another met her on the porch.

"Ms. Share?"

"Yes, Officer." She gestured to the fire truck with her free hand. "Did he set something on fire?"

"No, Ma'am. Dispatching the fire department to a call is standard procedure."

"Oh."

She considered his use of the term: *call*. This was "a call." The plethora of emergency vehicles and personnel outside her home was "a call."

"Did you stop to purchase a bird on the way home?"

She shook her head slightly as she set Sunny's travel cage close to the wall. "No. This is just the travel cage for my pet. I dropped him at a friend's house after work."

The officer made a note of that.

"Could you tell me when was the last time you spoke with Mr. Dos?"

"Umm, this morning. Before I left for work." She glanced to the closed garage door, thankful to see it hadn't been open all day. "In the garage."

"In the garage?" he asked.

She looked at his eyes, taking in the depth of the wrinkles in the corners. This man had seen worse things than a crazy alcoholic boyfriend who wanted to keep tabs on the absent workaholic girlfriend. "Yes. He wanted to continue an argument after I'd left the condo, so he came out to the garage to do so. Is he still here? Inside?"

"Yes, Ma'am. Deputy Rodriguez is speaking with him. That was the last time you spoke?"

"I sent him an email later in the morning. He needed some information to send to the hospital, but we didn't talk then. Just...just the email."

The officer made a note of that, too. "Mr. Dos seems distraught over the state of your relationship."

Melody felt the need for Aleve. Rather than start digging through her purse for medication, she pressed her fingers against her temple. "Our relationship is ending. He told me this morning that he'd be gone by the time I got home this evening, but he has made that kind of statement before."

"He asked us to call you to make sure you were coming home. I take it you're usually home before seven o'clock?"

"Not really. I work long hours. Crazy boss. Crazy company. But I told him this morning that I'd be late getting home. That was before he threatened to leave, though, so I can see how he'd forget." She recognized that she made an excuse for Larry, and squinted at the officer. Did he recognize it, too? "Sir, is he sober? I mean, will he be able to drive anywhere tonight? Will he try to take my car? He has a set of keys to my car, but he's not insured anymore."

The officer looked genuinely surprised. "We can't let him drive, no. Ma'am, he asked our dispatcher to find you and make sure you were safe. But the things he stated while on the phone with our dispatcher led her to send us here." The officer gestured toward the street. "All of us."

Melody nodded. This was starting to make sense. Larry was off his rocker, as she'd told Julia on the phone this morning. The police dispatcher recognized it and sent the team of responders.

"Could you tell me about the disagreement you had this morning?" he asked.

"Umm, this morning? It was ridiculous. In hindsight, I don't know why I tried again or why I thought he would take the matter seriously this time or why I thought it was reasonable to let him know what our actual expenses are. See, he quit his job a while back and last week, he asked me to show him what his half of our expenses would be.

"Then yesterday, the hospital where he was Sunday morning requested proof that he has no income and proof of his expenses, so I told him this morning that he needed to send the list to them.

"When he asked about it before, he wanted the list to include the HOA dues and the cable bill. You know? It was part of a larger conversation about how to save up for a new car for him when we talked about it last week. It made sense to me at the time. This morning, it was part of a larger conversation about showing the hospital that he can't pay them thousands of dollars.

"Anyway, I brought it up again this morning because he has to get in touch with the hospital or he's going to end up with a huge medical bill. I shouldn't have. It made him mad. I think he forgot why I had the list last time. He thought I was giving him an invoice. Both times.

"He sees it as some kind of ultimatum. So this morning, he decided that I was telling him to pay up or get out. Again. He said if I went to work without resolving it, he would be gone by the time I got home."

"And by 'be gone,' what did he mean?" the officer asked.

The extra implication struck Melody squarely when the officer said it. "Oh my God," she said. "I…I don't know. I thought he was going to leave. I thought he'd call a cab or Jenny, his sponsor from AA. I thought I'd come home to find him packed up and moved out. Are you saying he tried to kill himself? Is he okay?"

"Ma'am, he didn't try to kill himself, but he has made some distressing statements. Mr. Dos is distraught about the state of your relationship, and I think he is a danger to himself. We're going to take him to the hospital for observation for tonight."

Melody stared at the officer for a moment.

"Ma'am?"

"What does that mean?" she asked.

"We're just going to have a doctor take a look at him, have someone talk to him."

Melody nodded. "Did you take away his gun?"

"Yes, Ma'am. We've taken his weapon into custody. We'll hold it until he's cleared."

She understood that, and she was relieved. Considering the random mixing of blood pressure medication with vodka and pain killers left Larry defending their home against shadowy invaders more often than she cared to share with the officer, it was best that loaded weapons be taken to a secure facility offsite.

"Mr. Dos told us that you have a gun as well?"

"Yes, I do. It's not on the premises."

"Why is that?"

"I have a friend holding it and my ammunition for me at this time," she said. "I didn't think it was safe to have in the house given…given Larry's hallucinations lately."

The officer frowned. "And what hallucinations are those?"

"He sees things. I'm sure the doctor he speaks with can help him with that. I can make sure you get a bag of his medications."

They stared at each other for a moment, and she hoped he wouldn't pry.

"What kinds of things does he see?"

"Umm…you know…things that too much medication can cause you to see."

"You're saying he's over-medicated?"

"Probably. But I'm not a doctor."

The officer managed to get more information from her than she wanted to share. Interrogation technique, she thought, as she spilled the locations she knew of the vodka bottles hidden in the guest bathroom, the tool chest in the garage, his coat sleeves in the den closet, the egg crate under the den window. By the time their conversation was complete, she felt as if she'd betrayed Larry. Watching the officers guide him to the cruiser in the driveway, she noticed he'd put on clothes at some point during the day. "Poor guy," she mumbled.

"Mr. Dos will be under doctor supervised detox for seventy-two hours," the officer said. "At that time, he'll be released to a rehabilitation center for a twenty-eight-day program, if they have a bed available." The man handed her a business card. "If you have any questions, don't hesitate to call me."

Like a whirlwind, the last cruiser drove away and Melody found herself standing behind the closed condo door. Silence held her. It was as if the presence of stillness had been waiting for the opportunity, and rushed up to wrap its body around her. She closed her eyes, half expecting Larry to shout something from the living room or the bedroom, demanding to know why she was just standing there doing nothing. But silence held her more tightly, comforting her with a warm embrace that left her just enough room to breathe in, and out, and breathe in, and out.

Because she had arrived home shortly before eight o'clock and the interrogation from the officer had lasted almost an hour, it was nearly nine o'clock when she closed and locked the door on the world outside. She stood there so the sense of peace and calm could seep into her as the dusk of evening seeped into the condo. The thermostat clicked and the air conditioner whirred into obedience.

Soft sounds of frogs reminded her that summer lizards would poop on her car windshield overnight if she left it outside the garage, but she didn't care. In fact, she opened her eyes and reached forward to flick up the switch that turned on the porch light. She would attract bugs for the frogs and lizards to munch on.

Turning to face the darkening condo, she grinned almost maniacally. "I can sleep tonight!" She walked into the kitchen. "I can eat whatever I want for dinner!" She was about to reach for the refrigerator when she stopped and whirled toward the living room. "I can watch whatever I want on TV!"

She caught herself giggling. "Omigosh. I don't know what to do first."

Then she checked the clock for real. She needed to find free boxes and buy as much packing tape as she could afford. If Larry was gone for three days, she had three days to pack. She picked up her purse and called Julia while she headed out to her car.

Chapter 15

"Wow. Mels. What are you on today?" Betty asked.

Melody didn't look up from the computer screen, but asked, "Whaddya mean?"

"You're glowing. Did you get laid last night? Larry finally get Mr. Winky to work again?"

"Nice." Melody pressed "save" on her work file so she could be distracted without losing anything, and picked up her phone. "I was up until nearly 2:00 a.m. packing clothes and books and kitchen items into boxes from Publix and Wal-Mart. Larry's in the hospital."

"Again?" Betty asked, lowering herself to the plastic chair. She skipped over the packing part of the conversation that didn't interest her.

"This time it's different. He's on an actual psych hold or something. Listen to this." Melody tapped through the screens and security number on her smart phone while Betty talked.

"There's something seriously wrong with you. You shouldn't be giddy over the fact your boyfriend is in the looney bin."

"Hey, he did it to himself. He called the freakin' police because he thought I was late coming home from work yesterday. Here. Listen."

Melody pushed the speaker icon and held the phone up. After a second of silence, a low, almost demonic voice spoke in slow, measured beats. "Melody. I know you're screening your calls. I know you're avoiding me. You had me Baker Acted. This is the lowest thing you've ever done. I won't forget it."

They listened to the strange, underwater sounds of a phone's handset being bumped and fumbled around before the call disconnected.

Betty sat back in the white lawn chair in Melody's office with her mouth hanging open and her brow contorted in disgust. "Oh my gawd, Mels. What does Baker Acted mean?"

"That's when a doctor decides you're a danger to yourself or others and uses the Baker Act to put you on a psych hold for observation for a few days."

"So how did you do that?"

"*I* didn't. The cops did. And *that*, my friend, is the bullshittery I've been dealing with for the past nine months."

"How long is he gonna be inna hospital?"

"The officers who took him away last night said he'd be there three days and then they'd ship him to a rehab place for a month. Now, he's always turned down the twenty-eight-day program thing; he won't stay sober that long or thinks I'll leave him if he's in a facility that long. Whatever. So I figure I have until Friday night to get packed and get out. But I can't move into the apartment until Saturday. So I filed the paperwork this morning at the courthouse to get a three-day restraining order, which I learned is the easiest to get. When it gets approved, that clock starts ticking. So I'll have time to get moved this weekend without him harassing me the whole time."

As if ignoring all the logistics and planning that went into the information Melody had just thrown at her, Betty said, "So you'll have to break your lease."

"Yes, I will. I spoke to the landlord and she's not willing to let me off the lease because Larry has no way to pay the rent on his own. So I'd be stuck, unless I just screw up my rental history. Ms. Dirvish has already accepted me to move into the efficiency apartment this weekend, and thank you for connecting me with her, so screwing up my rental history won't affect me right now. And, at this point, I'm willing to screw up my rental history to keep from waking up with a bullet going through my brain in the middle of the night."

"Mels. I don't believe it's that bad."

Melody didn't hold it against Betty for not listening to her worsening stories for the past nine months; Betty didn't listen to anyone for comprehension.

"Let's go drinking tonight," Betty suggested.

Melody appreciated the gesture, but wanted to go back to her fortress of solitude and continue packing. "Maybe during one of our break days?" she countered. "I have more packing to do. And I want to sleep tonight. It's so peaceful sleeping without Larry randomly waking me up."

"For sex," Betty said, nodding as if she totally understood.

"No," Melody laughed. "Just waking me up. He has this bizarre habit of reaching over and touching me while he's watching TV, and I can sleep through the light and the noise of the TV, but it freaks me out when his hand lands on me and wakes me up. Tonight, I want to sleep with nothing landing on me."

"You complain a lot," Betty said, as if she just decided it. "Do you think he complains this much about you?"

"I honestly don't care. His opinion of me probably shifts from hour to hour, depending on his blood alcohol ratio content whatever. After his accident Friday, he told me that he thinks tons of people would come to my funeral because I'm so great, and then he turns around and tells me I'm a big baby that no one can stand to be around. Go figure."

"He's planning your funeral? That's at least a little bit scary."

"No, not planning." She wasn't sure why she felt the need to reassure Betty that Larry wasn't working out the specifics of her funeral, as if defending him against slander. "He was thinking about death after his accident because it could've been so much worse. He started by telling me no one would go to his funeral; he has no friends who care. That sort of thing."

"That's kinda messed up," Betty said.

"Agreed."

"So did you tell him you'd be there?" Betty asked.

"Yeah, but I just wanted to get off the subject."

"So you lied to him."

"I kinda had to. I wanted to get off the subject. Like now."

"No kidding," Betty said, missing Melody's hint. "Funerals are not really romantic conversation."

Melody laughed slightly. "Romantic conversation. I don't think Larry's had a romantic conversation in his life. He asked me if I expected a lot of people at my funeral."

"Ugh. What did you tell him?"

"I don't know…something about whoever's still around."

"Do you ever think about that?" Betty asked, lowering her voice as if this was a serious conversation to discuss.

"No."

"I mean, what if we outlive all our friends?" Betty was onto a philosophical theme now. "Who comes to our funerals?"

"Our kids. Let's move on," Melody suggested.

"But neither of us has kids."

"Then we have to make a pact. Betty, if I die first, you come to my funeral. If you die first, I come to yours. Can we stop talking about funerals and death now?"

"One more thing. What music do you want at yours?"

Melody stopped working on the file she wished to return to on her computer and turned to fully face Betty across the desk. "Seriously? Are you seriously asking me what music I want at my funeral? We're barely forty years old."

"Speak for yourself! I'm only thirty-five."

"And you've strengthened the point I'm trying to make," Melody said. "This is not something we have to worry about right now. I have work to do."

"There's always work to do. Let me *in*, Mels. What music?"

"Okay. I want my funeral at midnight of the new moon when it's darkest out, and I want only baroque chamber music played by a string quartet."

Betty stared at her for a minute. "I was being serious."

Melody shrugged. "At this point in my life, that sounds pretty good."

"That's really dark, Mels. Really dark."

"And what do you want?"

"I want old school songs," Betty said. "The Pussycat Dolls and Prince and maybe some Snoop Dogg. It should be a party."

"I'm not dancing on your grave."

Betty threw her head back and laughed, but this time, Melody couldn't tell if it was fake or not.

"So what do you think Lair wants?" Betty asked. "What's his idea of a good funeral, you know, if anyone shows up?"

Melody shook her head. "I don't know. All he likes are drinking songs."

"Like country songs?"

"Yes. But classic rock stuff, too. *One Bourbon, One Scotch, One Beer.* And that's the version he prefers, by the way. The one by George Thorogood. I doubt he even knows about the previous bluesy ones. I think he likes the *Tequila* song, also."

"No one can actually sing those songs, you know."

Melody snorted. "Ladies and Gentlemen, *not* in your hymnals…"

Betty laughed again, and this time she was genuine.

"You know, that *One Beer* song isn't really about drinking," Betty said. "It's about getting revenge."

Melody frowned. "Are you serious? That would be so fitting…"

"I don't follow."

"It doesn't matter. Larry has this propensity for wanting to go after those who have wronged him in the past. He's got a list. If the song he likes so much is really about revenge *and* drinking, it's perfect."

"We do need to go out drinking," Betty said.

"Not anytime soon," Melody said. "There are too many people wallowing in alcoholism and addiction in this town for my comfort. I'd rather go to a quiet dinner where no one's judging me for what I'm eating or what I'm spending or what I'm talking about or what I'm wearing…"

As her thought and voice trailed away, she realized Betty was staring.

"You've got a lot of issues, Mels."

Chapter 16

By Thursday evening, Melody heard back from the law firm Betty had recommended. While she disassembled Sunny's flight cage so she could fit the pieces in the back of her car, she consulted by speakerphone with one of the research assistants frankly about the situation, letting the woman know her intent was not to get rich.

"I want you guys to make the money while you safeguard me against being sued. I have this horrible feeling that the family Larry hit will seek a settlement, and I don't know what will happen to me after that. The insurance company needs to be found liable for everything so I can be found innocent of everything."

"That's not really how it works," the research assistant told her.

"Maybe not, but can we get it to work *something* like that? I want to be protected from stuff coming back to haunt me a year from now. Also, the company I work for sent out an email this afternoon trying to downplay its liability for rampant identity theft within the company. You wanna hit that, too? I mean, I don't want to make money off of this. I just want it to *not* come back to bite me a year or two from now. In fact, my identity has already been stolen. I'm one of the employees who had her personal information taken from our CFO's laptop."

"What?" the woman asked. "Did someone hack the company's system? Get through an inadequate firewall?"

"I think a combination of things happened," Melody spoke toward the smart phone on the couch. "The CFO's laptop was stolen during a burglary at the headquarters office in Chicago. But no one at this location was told about the break-in. And no one beyond corporate management knew what was stolen. So no one had any idea that personal information was potentially floating around until a couple of us in this office had credit problems hit us."

"Are you serious? Is there any evidence of any of this?" the assistant asked.

"Besides all the cars we own from dealerships around the Chicago area? There's plenty. We have police reports out of Chicago for the burglary now. And now there's this email that went to the entire company database telling us how improbable it is that there's any connection between multiple identity misappropriations and theft of Mr. Andrew Roll's office equipment."

"And he's the CFO?"

"Yep."

"Can you forward the email to me?" the woman asked.

"I printed it out here when I got home. I think our server tracks outgoing messages. The company I work for defines paranoia…as it pertains to its employees."

"This sounds like a slam-dunk, but not necessarily a high-dollar payout."

"I'm not trying to hire a shark to make money for myself," Melody said. "That's not my goal. My goal is to clean up my record and keep it clean. Also, I don't want to get fired. I need my paycheck."

"Most of us do," the woman said. "But our motto is to get paid after our client gets paid. Did Betty tell you some of the settlements we've achieved for clients in Collier County alone? We don't really work on cases for the joy of seeing the little guy come out with nothing."

"But I don't want anything other than a clean slate."

"That sounds very altruistic of you. Let's set up a meeting and go over what can be done and what can't be done in these cases. From what you've said, the insurance company case has some merit. We can look at the identity theft situation and see what merit is there as well. And then we can discuss altruism in all its forms. How does that sound?"

"Sounds great. The company I work for is having a mandatory break next week. Can we set the meeting during that time? Then I won't have to take more time off work."

"I'll have the receptionist set that up with you. Could I…could I ask you a strange question?"

Melody felt her heart sink a little and heard herself answering, "sure."

"It's just that I don't often do consultations with clients who aren't after a big payout. I wonder, do you believe in reincarnation?"

That wasn't the question Melody was expecting. She wiped her hands on her thighs and looked at the phone. "Umm, well, no."

"In that mythos, there's an idea that doing good deeds in this life makes the path easier for yourself in the next life. Your comment about cleaning the slate brought it to mind."

"Maybe I'm just letting my next life off the hook."

* * *

Melody sat on the couch with her phone to her ear later that night. She spoke to Julia about her friend's flight schedule the next day.

"The sheriff's office called today and they'll serve the restraining order on Larry at the hospital tomorrow."

"Doesn't he get out tomorrow?" Julia asked.

"Not until late in the day. After 7:00. It's a seventy-two hour hold for a Baker Act. I'm not clear on when the clock started on that—if it was when the police took him away around 7:30 Tuesday night or later when the doctor saw him and made the pronouncement. I don't know. All I know is they're going to get to him with the order before then, and that's great. So you and I can sleep here tomorrow night, and then move things Saturday."

"How much do you have packed?"

"Ugh. Not enough. I'm overwhelmed. Moving wasn't on the radar for another three months. I have to figure out how to cram only my special belongings into a tiny studio apartment. .and what to donate…and what to put in a storage unit…if I can get it to a storage unit."

"You're stressing out. Why don't you get some sleep and we'll tackle it all tomorrow together."

"That sounds good. I miss Sunny. If I'd known this place was going to be safe, I could have kept him with me."

"He's okay where he is. Wouldn't all the packing and stuff cause him stress?"

"Maybe," Melody said.

"So he's being spoiled by your friend. It's all good."

Melody let that soothe her. "Okay. I'll see you at the airport."

"10:00 your time," Julia said.

Chapter 17

Melody drove to Southwest Florida International Airport the next morning with bottles of cold water and a big bag of gummy bears. She pulled up to the correct door on the lower level of the terminal and waited all of a minute before Julia popped out with her suitcase.

A few people nearby looked at them when they emitted the sounds of hamsters stuck in a blender. Typically, such noises came out of young girls, maybe co-eds, not women of forty years of age. Because they were, technically, parked by the curb, they couldn't dally without upsetting a security officer. Melody lifted the trunk hood and scooted a box that had slid out of place out of the way. They lifted Julia's suitcase into the trunk and Julia pointed at the box. "Already?"

"Just a couple vital heirlooms. Grandma's teacup, Grandpa's Bible, favorite book, stuff I fear losing."

"Got it," Julia said. They'd been friends long enough that Julia didn't need further explanation. "You're not paranoid if they're really out to get you," she said.

"Exactly."

"You look great," Julia said, as they moved to the front of the car.

"Are you lying to me?" Melody asked.

"No. You look really good. I expected you to be strung out and pale and stuff. Maybe some chocolate drool on your chin. This is good to see instead. Ooooo…are these gummy bears? Did you bring me gummy bears?"

"I did."

"How are you keeping yourself together enough to bring me gummy bears?" Julia was tearing the bag open while Melody pulled them away from the curb.

"Seatbelt," Melody said.

"Have you heard anything from the hospital? From the cops?"

"Only thing coming out of the hospital is scary voice mail messages from Larry. I'm afraid to answer his calls. Actually afraid. I don't want the Tourette's tirade."

"No kidding," Julia said. "Did you hide his gun so he can't come after you with it once he gets back into the condo?"

"Oh, the cops took it into custody. When they put a person under a psych hold, they confiscate loaded weapons."

"Thank God that's a thing," Julia said. "People think there are no checks and balances, but that right there? A check and balance."

"I don't know how he passed the background check for the thing in the first place, other than someone got his record expunged. You won't believe what I found about his background when I was packing *my* papers from the den."

Julia bit the head off a gummy bear. "Lay it on me."

"I found court transcripts from that domestic violence thing he went through in North Carolina."

Julia snorted. "Let me guess. Not exactly the way he described it?"

"Not exactly. Larry has his own way of describing things. I get that lawyers can make things sound however they need to, but I read part of the transcript, and it's the woman he was living with, Carrie, on the stand, under oath, telling how he had her trapped in the basement for two hours after he hit so hard she couldn't hear out of one ear. But she could hear out of the other ear, and all she could hear was him screaming profanities at her for two hours."

Julia didn't respond for a minute, and when she did, she wasn't being sarcastic any longer. "How did he get away with that?"

"He knew people. He left the state." Melody checked her side mirror before switching lanes for her turn. "He finished his parole or whatever down here in Florida and he's been going through women down here. I didn't realize it...I didn't realize that the lady he lived with down here, the one who got him fired from that mechanics place, I can't think of her name now, but he refers to her as a snake, she had locked him out of their place because she was tired of him drinking after work, and when he couldn't get in one night, he ended up getting fired the next day. I always found that story pretty strange, right? But I get it now. The drinking. The woman locking him out. He probably wasn't locked out. He was probably too drunk to get the door open."

"Or you're just believing what he told you, and it didn't happen that way at all."

"Or that," Melody agreed.

"I wonder if this snake woman is the only lady here in Florida that he's lived with other than you."

"I know he was living with Jenny, his AA sponsor, when I met him, but supposedly she was just a sponsor, not a romantic partner. He really doesn't like her. Calls her a phony and a hypocrite. That sort of thing."

"It sounds like he has a problem with women," Julia said.

"Truth. But I have to agree with his opinion of Jenny."

"Because you keep sticking up for him?" Julia asked.

Melody paused. "I don't think I'm sticking up for him. Am I?"

"Everything you say is with this overlay of 'poor Larry.' He's got you in his martyr mindset. He's not the martyr he's made himself out to be. From the outside, looking in, I can tell you, this guy is a manipulator."

Melody nodded at that. "Okay. I can see that. But this Jenny woman really is a piece of work. She's supposed to be a sponsor in Alcoholics Anonymous, but she does drugs and sells prescription pain meds to the highest bidder."

Julia gasped. "How does that work?"

"Right? Apparently, she considers herself sober if she's not drunk. The drugs don't count."

Julia snorted. "Stupid."

"Things are coming together now," Melody said. "I hadn't thought of it, but Larry probably gets pills from Jenny. That's why the doctor put him on Buprenowhatsit."

"What?"

"I can't remember the whole name unless I'm reading it on a prescription label," Melody said. "There's a drug…starts with Bupren. It's to treat you when you're detoxing from opiate withdrawals, when you're coming off opiates. When Larry had his accident last Friday—"

"His accident?"

"Oh, yeah, I didn't tell you about that part. I was so focused on his last drinking binge and the stuff since then. He wrecked his car Friday."

"Was he drunk driving?"

"I think so. I haven't gotten the full story out of anyone. But the insurance company canceled our policy."

"You're kidding."

"Lemme start from the beginning. Friday, he wrecked his car. And let me also say that I'm worried about a boy that was in the car he hit. I want to check into that without getting myself stuck in a lawsuit of some kind."

"I'll make a note," Julia said.

"Anyway, then Saturday, I picked him up at the hospital and the doctors had given him a stack of scripts to fill. Two of them were for detox drugs. A couple were for pain. Not a good combination. Especially not a good combination if Jenny has been supplying him with extra drugs on the side. Saturday afternoon, we went to dinner with my friends Inari and Mark, but Larry was too moody to eat, so he pitched a fit and drank beer and Saki, on top of the pain meds. By the time we got home, he was passed out. By that night, he was all kinds of messed up. I took him to the emergency room, which is actually a longer story than that, but I got him to the emergency room, and they cleaned him up a bit by Sunday morning. Then Sunday night we both got food poisoning. Then you know he threatened Sunny Monday night."

Julia shook her head. "I can't believe you do all this crap for him."

"Not anymore," Melody said. "Not any…"

She let her words fade on the air as she brought the car to a slow stop in the middle of Northwest 5th Street. In front of her condo, a taxicab's passenger door opened. Her cell phone chimed in its cradle on the dash. Betty's name appeared on the screen.

* * *

Melody pulled the car into the first driveway on the right, and swiped the phone.

"Hey, Betty."

"Mels. You *won't* believe who was here this morning."

"Let me guess," Melody said.

"Larry came here and was demanding someone drive him up to your condo. He talked to Ken Bilso for like half an hour. Where are you?"

"I'm a few houses down from my condo."

Betty's melodramatic gasp filled the car. Julia rolled her eyes.

"Mels, he's really mad. Don't go home."

"Thank you, Betty."

"You bet, Sistah. Dr. Mason needs me. Gotta go."

The phone disconnected.

"Please tell me that's not your support system down here," Julia said.

"Betty's focused on climbing up the boss's ass and finding a guy to marry...not necessarily finding the guy up the boss's ass, but you get what I mean." Melody spoke absently, not filtering the words passing her lips. She watched Larry climb from the taxi with a paper grocery bag in his arms. One of the reassuring things about having Julia in the car was not having to filter what she said, though. Melody could have her observation skills locked on Larry while her mouth spewed commentary, and there was no worry about being judged. No games. "Betty's not looking for lifelong friends. She's more interested in who will go drinking with her tonight and then who will go home with her afterward."

"What's he doing?" Julia asked.

"I can't tell," Melody said. "He's going to the front door, but the taxi's not leaving."

"Do you think he's just dropping that bag off and then leaving again?"

"That would be awesome..."

"As long as it's not a bomb," Julia said under her breath.

They both chuckled at the sardonic humor, and then watched quietly for a minute. They listened to the whir of the air conditioner while they waited for Larry to reappear. Melody heard Julia's hand crinkle the gummy bear bag, and turned her head to give a questioning glance at the treats.

Julia grinned. "They're addictive."

When Melody's phone chimed, it made them both jump.

104

"For Pete's sake," Melody muttered.

Larry's name appeared on the screen.

"I don't think you should answer that," Julia said.

"I'm so glad Sunny's not in there," Melody said.

"I'm so glad his gun's not in there," Julia said. "Can we go to the police station and let them know where he is?"

"That's a great idea."

"That's why I'm here. To provide the great ideas."

Melody put the car in reverse and they were several streets away before the phone chimed to signal a voice mail message.

"Is he calling again?" Julia asked.

"No. That's the voice mail alert."

"Holy crap, that's a long message."

"I can only imagine," Melody sighed.

"Let's listen to it with the police."

"I think I'd like to hear it first," Melody said. "God only knows what kind of crap he's saying."

At the next red light, she pressed the buttons to release the message to the space in the car, and they listened to Larry's low, angry, slow voice.

"Melody. I see you've packed up to leave me for another man. After all I've done for you…while you spent all your time on your career and ignored our relationship for the past year, you've packed the things I bought for you so you can leave me with a lease you know I can't afford on my own. I'm at our home and I need you to get back here to pay the cab driver because you weren't at work to drive me here yourself. The man you've been screwing at work said you were at home today. I guess you lie to him, too. You need to get back here right now and take care of the cat and then have the decency to talk to me about this situation. Unless you're too much of a coward and a bitch to talk to my face. I'll be waiting for you at our home."

Melody pulled the car into the police station parking lot as the message finished and Julia quietly said, "Yeah, you're gonna need to play that for the cops."

"What? It sounds like I'm a cretin! He implies I'm having an affair with a guy at work."

"*That* is a crazy person rambling in a crazy way," Julia said. "The police will perceive that."

"He says that I'm stealing things he bought for me."

"Do you not hear that it's deranged?" Julia asked.

"Well, yes, *I* know it's crazy, but doesn't it sound like he's laying the groundwork to make me look like the one who's gone around the bend? He's accusing me of stealing things, saying I've neglected our relationship, implying I'm cheating on him—"

"You're smarter than this," Julia said. "Play the message for the cops. Show them the restraining order and tell them where he is. They'll get him out of there."

Melody nodded. "Okay. Okay."

"Ready? We're going into this station and we're solving this problem."

* * *

Deputy Sheriff Don Broy raised one eyebrow during the second sentence of the recording. By the end of the message, he had pulled his keys from the top drawer of his desk, and handed the Court Order of Protection from Melody to the assistant seated nearby. "Make a copy of this right now, please," he said to the young man. "Meet me out front with it and the original."

He gestured for the ladies to follow him as he walked to the front doors of the station. "I want you to go relax at a coffee shop for about an hour. It shouldn't take that long, but let's be on the safe side. Now, you said the only weapon has been confiscated?"

"That's right," Melody answered.

"There are no other weapons in the house?"

"Well...kitchen knives. He usually has a pocketknife. But he just got out of the hospital so I don't think he'd have that on him. But, no, no more guns."

"Very good. Rocko," he barked down the corridor. "We've got a call."

A call, Melody thought. Again.

The blur and flurry of papers and officers and keys confused her for a few moments. She became aware of Julia's hand on her arm, guiding her to a bench outside. The heat of late morning couldn't be abated by a shade tree, but the tree gave a valiant effort.

"You wanna go to Dunkin Donuts?" Julia asked.

"In a minute. I think I'm freaking out."

"That's totally understandable. You wanna just breathe for a while?"

"I'd like that," Melody said.

After the past week of constant strife and movement, Melody felt almost uncomfortable sitting still, but wanted to try it. She closed her eyes, as if that would help bring her nerves under control. It only took a moment of rest to recognize the futility of it.

Being in one place, immobile, was unproductive and unwise. She needed to be packing a box for her move into a new home the next day. She needed to be assembling evidence to provide the attorney for the meeting on Monday. She needed to be planning how to fend off creditors while

106

attorneys worked on cases. She needed to be researching security systems for her new apartment. She needed to visit the post office to get her mail forwarding unlisted and a post office box set up. She needed to buy a burner phone to carry for emergencies.

The ideas jumbled in her mind like falling dominoes. She could even hear them clattering in her brain. As if trying to get out of her own head, she opened her eyes. Before her, the parking lot wavered with heat and a pair of yellow butterflies danced around one another about four feet above the grass. They fluttered in a random, frantic panic of egg-making foreplay, circling and flirting as they crisscrossed the edge of the parking lot. She felt that same fluttering in her chest. Random and frenetic.

"I can't just sit here," she finally said.

"Would you like to go somewhere with AC?" Julia asked.

"Let's go to the post office. I need to get a post office box. Let's do that."

"Excellent idea," Julia said in affirmation. "Do you want to make a list first? We can make a list while we sit here."

"No, we can make a list while we stand in line at the post office."

"Okay. Let's go."

Chapter 18

Saturday started earlier than either Melody or Julia wanted it to. They'd accomplished much of their ambitious list Friday afternoon, and returned to the condo to find Larry had wrecked the place.

"Umm," Julia said upon entering the condo. "Is this how you were packing things?"

"Oh my. No. No, I…" Melody's heart sank within her as she looked around at torn and upended boxes. A box of silverware had apparently been thrown across the kitchenette because forks, spoons, butter knives, and various utensils were all over the floor. In front of the busted television they saw a mound of torn books and covers and pages and scraps. "Oh no," Melody said, worried about what she'd find in the den—the room with the expensive-stuff-to-replace.

She glanced around that room, taking a quick inventory of the smashed computer screen, the smashed printer, the smashed shredder, and the smashed CD player. She didn't see the backup drive or modem, and hoped those were merely knocked to the floor somewhere.

She walked back to the living room and looked at the debris. A lot of anger had created this mess. It reminded her of an after-school special that taught of the crime and evils of vandalism. She felt vandalized. "I'm going to need more tape," Melody sighed.

"That's the spirit. We'll fix this." Julia scooted silverware with her foot to create a path through the kitchen area so she could reach the sink. As if she instinctively knew what her friend kept beneath it, she opened the cabinet door and took out a box of black Hefty trash bags. "Are you comfortable with me throwing away things that are destroyed?"

"Yes."

Julia set her purse in the sink. "I'll go get my suitcase. You pick a spot for me to begin."

They found all of Sunny's food—all of it—dumped in the master bathroom toilet. There was so much that pellets were even poured onto the tile floor.

"That's a lot of hate," Julia observed.

"I'm so glad Sunny wasn't here," Melody sobbed.

"No time for that," Julia said. "Do you have some gloves? Plastic gloves? This isn't going to flush."

"You do *not* have to unclog the toilet. Let me deal with—"

"It's a project I can handle," Julia said. "You keep throwing away destroyed things and taping up boxes. I can do this."

Thus a late Friday work-night became an early Saturday work-morning. Melody turned on the shower and stepped back, expecting something gross to come out of the showerhead. Apparently, Larry hadn't thought of that. After a quick shower, she got back to packing and cleaning while Julia got herself cleaned up for the day. When Julia stepped into the living room, she asked, "Did you know there's a vodka bottle in the toilet tank in there?"

Melody giggled. "I'm not surprised."

"It made me think of something."

Melody tossed a pillow into a Hefty bag. "Donation bag," she announced. "What are you thinking?"

"Well...after you move out, Larry can come back in here. He can live here until the lease is up, right?"

"If he pays the rent."

"Well, he's not going to clean up. Look what he did yesterday. Do you think you should warn the landlord? Do you think we should clean up now, take pictures of a good, clean place, and then you have proof that you left it in good condition?"

"I like the idea of getting proof," Melody said. "But the landlord has already told me she's not letting me out of the lease. She'll have to evict Larry after I go. So I'm going to have the broken lease on my rental history, and I think, if I understand it right, that the eviction of him shows up on my history, too, because we're both on the lease."

"What a wenchball. Did you tell her what he was doing?"

"Yes," Melody sighed. "She doesn't care. It's business. She wants her monthly payment."

"If he kills you, she doesn't get a monthly payment."

"I kinda suggested that. I don't think she was buying it."

"What a wench," Julia repeated under her breath. Aloud she said, "Maybe she's heard it as an excuse in the past. You know, people trying to get out of a lease or something."

"I don't know. All I know is business shouldn't come before someone's safety."

"I agree," Julia said. "Is this his?"

Melody looked at the misshapen board Julia held up.

"Yes. Leave that."

"What is it?" Julia asked.

"It's a TV tray. He won't sit at the table to eat. So he uses that tray to eat in bed. In his chair. On the toilet."

"Ewww. He eats on the toilet?"

"Yep. Very strange. I used to think that's why he was sick so often. You know, he'd get these stomach problems all the time. He was always complaining about his stomach being upset and he'd be nauseated constantly. I told him to stop eating in the bathroom because of germs." Melody stood upright with a bag in one hand and gestured like she was throwing confetti with the other. "Flecks of feces."

"Gross," Julia said.

"Exactly? I mean, you know there's scientific proof of gross stuff every time a toilet flushes. Why on earth would a person eat in there? Anyway, I think now that his problem was a combination of the unsanitary eating and the stupid drinking."

"Still gross," Julia announced.

"I wonder why I never saw it."

"Because he's a manipulator. And an experienced drunk knows how to hide it."

The doorbell rang to signal the movers had arrived early.

"Ah, the expenses begin," Melody said.

"How did you get a truck on such short notice?"

"It's a van," Melody answered, picking her way around the neatly stacked boxes toward the front door. "And that's how. There were no trucks available on such short notice. We have a dude and his son and a van to move the large boxes that won't fit in my car."

When Melody opened the door, Larry pushed her back inside.

* * *

"You can't be here," Melody said.

"You have a lot of explaining to do," he barked at her, slamming the door behind him. He didn't stop advancing on her, but continued pushing her back with flat, open hands, quickly moving them into the house as he yelled. "A lot of explaining. Just what makes you think you can walk out on this relationship?"

As they reached the edge of the kitchenette, he saw Julia in the bedroom doorway, her phone already up to her ear.

The woman's presence obviously startled him. It interrupted his train of thought. He had to switch tactics. He moved his attention back to Melody, grabbing her arm.

"How dare you involve your friend in your betrayal? You apologize to your friend right now for getting her involved in this. Apologize!"

"Let go of me," she said, trying to wrench her arm free. She could hear Julia's voice saying words such as "he's in the house" and "violation of restraining order" behind her. She knew Julia was on the phone with the police. Smart lady. She'd called 9-1-1.

"A restraining order is just a piece of paper," Larry said. "It's just a sign that you've gone crazy. You're a lunatic. You've lost your mind. You're nuts if you think you can just walk out of this relationship and leave me with nothing. You have to help me find a place to live. You can't leave me with no place to live."

"The police are coming," Julia called out, as if to stop his tirade.

"Do you know what it costs to rent this place?" he continued as if he didn't hear her. "You picked the most expensive place in Florida to rent so I could never be on my own. And now you're going to leave me here? You're just like any other bitch on the streets, trying to keep me down. You owe me a place to live after all I've done for you. After all we've been through together. You're a heartless, selfish bitch if you think you can just walk out on me and leave me homeless with no way to take care of myself."

"The police are on their way," Julia announced again. "You better leave now."

"I'm not the one leaving," Larry fired back. "You have to let me move with you."

"There's no room for you," Melody said. "Now go. The police are coming and you have to go or you'll be arrested."

"Oh, you'd love that, wouldn't you? Get me arrested so you can have me kicked out of our home. That would look good for you, you crazy bitch."

"Get out," she snapped. "Go now!"

He glared at her, his eyes seeming to flash between hate and confusion. The women hesitated in the quiet, waiting to see what he was going to do. As if she channeled some inner force of calm, Melody lowered her voice to something soothing, something motherly, and said gently, "Larry. You have to get out of here before the police arrive."

He closed his eyes for a second, and when he opened them, the glassy stare she recognized from too many nights of his binge drinking met her. He released her arm and turned to leave without another word. It didn't seem as if he looked at anything around him as he walked toward the front door, but he stopped briefly, picked up a coffee mug from the counter, and then continued. He left without slamming the door. In fact, he didn't close it at all. He walked out, across the front lawn, leaving tracks from his sandals in the dew, and turned up the street toward the back exit of the neighborhood.

Melody didn't move right away, but Julia still had enough adrenaline to get to the front door, close it, lock it, and put the chain in place. She turned and leaned her back against the door, waiting for the police to arrive.

It took them fifteen minutes.

The ladies pointed in the direction Larry had walked, and the officers motored that way.

"This is why you need to get your gun back from your friend," Julia muttered. "Like the crazy man said, a restraining order is a piece of paper. It doesn't block Larry from walking in here. A bullet would."

They both jumped when the doorbell rang again.

This time, Melody looked through the peephole before opening the door to the worker standing on her front porch. He entered the condo calmly, and the ladies showed him which boxes to load.

Chapter 19

While the worker and his son moved the large boxes into Melody's new apartment, Julia took a box of cleaning supplies into the tiny bathroom to start scrubbing.

"What are you doing?" Melody asked. "You don't have to clean the bathroom. I can do that."

"You keep things moving out there. You know where you want stuff. I can clean this."

The ladies stared at the bathtub, which had a strange black film not just as a ring, but also along the sides and bottom.

"I wonder what was stored in here," Julia said.

"Stored or cooked?" Melody suggested. "There's a lot of methamphetamine in this part of Florida."

"Is meth black when it's cooked?"

Melody shrugged. "I've never seen it."

"Well, whatever this is, it's about to get cleaned." Julia took a can out of the box she'd set on the toilet seat. "With Borax. Where's the box of gloves?"

Once the movers left, the next thing Melody and Julia accomplished in her new apartment was assembling Sunny's flight cage by the ugly loveseat. Melody set up a food dish with new, fresh food she'd purchased on the way to move in.

"Now we can go get him," Melody said.

"Let's get rid of this crap first," Julia said, motioning toward the broken dish drainer and assorted plastic items in the sink, which was on the wall next to the ugly loveseat. "Did the landlord think you were going to use this broken stuff?"

"I don't know. I'm so tired, I don't care. I just want Sunny here so my life is back together."

"Okay. Let me dump this crap, and then we'll go get him."

Melody grabbed a black Hefty bag and held it open for Julia to throw odds-and-ends in. "We can throw this in the recycle center bin thingie on our way to Wendy's house," Melody said.

"I like that plan."

"Sunny's travel cage is still in the car."

By the end of Saturday, the ladies were exhausted. Again. Julia flopped on the bed to rest and Melody flopped on the loveseat. Sunny flopped in his cozy cave. And the three of them slept.

"Is he snoring?" Julia asked at one point.

"Sort of. He mutters in his sleep."

"That is adorable."

"It's a reassuring sound," Melody said. "Soft. Sweet."

* * *

The apartment was not ideal. It was small and cramped, and now it was filled with boxes that they would have to maneuver around to make the place livable. But it was safe. Being at the back of the property, butted up against a privacy fence, Melody felt confident Larry wouldn't find her easily. Security cameras around the property would alert anyone to trespassers. Even though it would be after the fact, the cameras would also record anything for court purposes later.

Sunday morning found them unpacking and sorting and stashing clothes and books all around the three-hundred-square-foot space. Melody was thankful for the closet and its door. A door meant she could block off some of the mess.

"You need more shelves," Julia announced.

"I think I can use the boxes as shelves for now. This lease is for a year. I need to rebuild for a year."

"Amen to that."

They looked around the tiny space and Sunny squeaked at them, as if asking why they had stopped moving.

"Let's do something not stressful for a couple hours," Julia said. "You need a break."

Melody chewed on her lower lip, which was an old, old habit from old days long ago. She recognized what she was doing, and stopped. "I don't know. There's a lot to do."

"There's always going to be a lot to do," Julia said. "You want to go to a movie? Go eat lunch?"

"I do need to get groceries."

"Going to the grocery store is not a fun and relaxing thing," Julia said. "We're going to take at least two full hours to do something that is not related to the advancement of your life. No stress. For at least two hours."

"And then can I go to the grocery store?"

Julia laughed a little bit. "Don't you have the next three days off work? That break the company forced you all to do?"

"Yeah. I guess the grocery can wait for after my appointment with the attorney tomorrow."

116

"Good Lord," Julia said. She flopped onto the loveseat to put on her shoes. "You're thinking about stressful things. Let's go to that place with the alligators and pigs and birds."

Melody thought about the concept—and comfort—Julia was suggesting. Her friend was right. They had accomplished a stressful move under stressful circumstances in a record amount of time. She finally had positive goals in motion in her life. She could actually relax knowing the time for rebuilding had officially begun. Finally.

"Are you talking about a zoo?" she asked Julia.

"No, the shell place. I want to buy a souvenir."

Melody giggled, and was thrilled to hear the sound. "To commemorate your exciting vacation helping me move boxes. I know how to show friends a good time when they come to Florida."

"This wasn't a *bad* time," Julia assured her. "It could have been a lot worse."

"You mean Larry could have shown up while we were packing? Oh, wait."

"Don't be a turd," Julia teased. "It could have been flooding while we were moving. It's summertime and you told me it usually rains like a constant monsoon here in the summertime. That would have been difficult. Trying to wade through water while moving boxes? Obnoxious."

"True. Hey, Sunny," Melody spoke to her little feathered friend.

He squeaked at her.

"We're gonna go to the zoo. We'll be back soon. Will you be my good bird while mommy's away?"

He squeaked the short, double-squeak that meant "bye-bye."

"That is adorable," Julia said.

"I'm so glad he's safe now," Melody said. She smiled at Sunny and lowered her voice to a whisper. "So glad we're safe."

\<The Beginning\>

Appendix

Violence against women includes more than physical abuse. Mental and psychological abuse may begin as something that is difficult to detect, but when a person feels unsafe, there are resources available to help her—or him.

The website www.womenshealth.gov includes an in-depth, secure resource site with information on how to know the signs of abuse, how to get help, how to plan a safe escape, how to file for a court order of protection (what's referred to as a restraining order in the story you've just read), how to help a friend, and links to specific help centers in all fifty states, plus the District of Columbia, Puerto Rico, and the Virgin Islands.

An additional excellent element about this site is a red "ESCAPE" button above the fold that you can click to immediately leave the site if your abuser should come up behind you. Also, the page is a women's health page, making it not immediately suspect to an abuser. But always remember to clear your browser history. The direct link to the page is https://www.womenshealth.gov/violence-against-women/get-help-for-violence/resources-by-state-violence-against-women.html.

In Kelsey's story, the character Melody had a pet to protect, and one that would have been problematic to take to a women's shelter. In North America, a system of women's shelters have started to take in pets along with the women who love them. Statistics have shown that women are more likely to stay in an abusive relationship to protect a pet; women fear their abusers harming a beloved pet in an act of retribution or as punishment for their leaving. Visit http://alliephillips.com/saf-tprogram/saf-t-shelters/ for a list, by state, of shelters that allow pets and resources for keeping pets and families together when escaping abuse.

The editor, Sandy Lender, attended an excellent presentation from a representative of Meg's House emergency shelter and supportive services for victims of domestic violence at Global Pet Expo in Orlando in 2017. The American Humane's Pets and Women's Shelters (PAWS)® Program advocates keeping domestic violence victims with their pets as often as possible. You can learn more at http://megshouse.org/programs/paws-pets-and-womens-shelter/.

Additional important resources

Office of Women's Health Helpline 1-800-994-9662 is open during business hours Monday through Friday

National Domestic Violence Hotline 1-800-799-7233 is always open

TDD 1-800-787-3224

In the United States 9-1-1 is the emergency number in almost every county now

If you live in the United Kingdom, the number to use for assistance is at Women's Aid, 0808 2000 247. The organization's website is http://www.womensaid.org.uk/

If you live in Australia, the number to use for assistance is 1800 737 732. The organization's website is http://www.1800respect.org.au/

If you live in Canada, a wide-reaching organization to contact is sheltersafe at www.ShelterSafe.ca/new-brunswick, and each province has individual resources listed at www.HotPeachPages.net/canada/index.html

Anywhere in the world, you can visit the resource guide at the International Directory of Domestic Violence Agencies at www.HotPeachPages.net, where information is available in a variety of languages.

Domestic violence is not limited to acts against women, and the resources listed herein offer links for men who have been victimized, as well.

About the Author

Kelsey Day has been raising parrots for decades and writing stories for as long as she can remember. Her dream since childhood has been to get the characters in her head introduced to the world.

About the Editor

Sandy Lender is a published author, magazine and book editor, copywriter, and publisher. With an English degree from Truman State University in Missouri, she works in the publishing and public relations fields during the day and writes fiction at night. Lender keeps house in Central Florida where her love of sea turtles, birds, and dragons keeps her imagination growing. ArcheBooks Publishing released her first fantasy novel in 2007, and she's released six books and a handful of short stories since then. She also publishes the parrot magazine *In Your Flock* four times a year. You can follow Sandy on facebook at Fantasy Author Sandy Lender. Reach out to her at publisher@inyourflock.com.